THE PERFECT SOLUTION

When her grandmother is ill, Emma Holberry steps in to run Holberry Animal Sanctuary, but she soon discovers it is on the brink of financial ruin. She decides to try and resolve the problems herself and finds the handsome new locum vet, Rick Delayne, an enormous support. A fund-raising ball is organised, but when Emma's fiancé, Nigel, drops out for business reasons, she is bitterly disappointed. At the ball, she welcomes Rick's company but is alarmed when she realises there is a growing attraction between them . . .

Books by Janet Cookson
in the Linford Romance Library:

QUEST OF THE HEART
MASQUERADE
TO LOVE FOR EVER
THE FAITHFUL HEART
A LOVE RECLAIMED
SPANISH TRYST
THE BEST MAN

JANET COOKSON

THE PERFECT SOLUTION

Complete and Unabridged

LINFORD
Leicester

First published in Great Britain in 2003

First Linford Edition
published 2004

British Library CIP Data

Cookson, Janet
    The perfect solution.—Large print ed.—
    Linford romance library
    1. Love stories
    2. Large type books
    I. Title
    823.9'14 [F]

    ISBN 1–84395–531–8

Published by
F. A. Thorpe (Publishing)
Anstey, Leicestershire

Set by Words & Graphics Ltd
Anstey, Leic-
Print-- --- --- in Great Britain by
-- --ernational Ltd., Padstow, Cornwall

This book is printed on acid-free paper

1

'It looks as though your grandmother's financial situation is even worse than we feared,' Nigel Hamilton said and a look of distaste passed over his handsome features as he dropped the invoice to re-join the stack on the table. 'And with her current health problems I don't see how she can keep the animal shelter open for very much longer.'

Sitting opposite him, Emma Holberry shifted in her seat and wished, not for the first time, that he could be a little less blunt when breaking bad news.

'That's hardly a message I can deliver at the moment, is it? Gran's recovering from a serious heart attack, she's making good progress, but stress would undo all that. I can't risk it, Nigel!'

He reached for her hand.

'I know how you feel, darling. I want

1

Martha to get well just as much as you but I don't see how concealing the truth from her will do any good. Things will only get worse and the shock will be all the greater when she does find out and she'll be furious with you for keeping her in the dark.'

There was much truth in what he said but Emma's firm response showed that she would not easily be swayed.

'I can see all that, but I know that now is not the time to break such devastating news.'

'Then what will you do?'

Her reply was succinct.

'Play for time. I'll pay the outstanding bills and then look to increasing our funding base.'

'All this could have been avoided if Martha had employed a properly qualified accountant to deal with her affairs.'

Emma bit back a retort that would have been too hasty. Inhabiting the well-ordered world of the law she knew that Nigel found it hard to come to terms with the precarious life her grandmother had chosen in order to fulfil her dream of looking after animals down on their luck.

In the end she settled for saying, 'Gran preferred the day-to-day work of looking after the animals, which meant leaving all the paperwork to one of the volunteers.'

'Who emigrated to Canada leaving a fine mess behind them. I'll sort it all into some sort of priority and then we can see about settling them.'

His choice of words was a welcome sign that, however reluctantly, he was willing to share the burden with her and Emma found herself breaking into a smile for the first time since they had embarked on this uncomfortable conversation. When he rose to go she placed a detaining hand on his arm.

'I really am grateful for all you're doing, darling. I'm like Gran, no head for figures. I'd be lost without your help.'

His head dipped to deposit a kiss on her cheek.

'That's only as it should be. After all, we'll be man and wife before too long, a day that can't come too soon for me.'

'Nor me,' Emma confirmed, then, before he could take the opening to ask her once more about setting a date, she rose and began to walk him towards the door. 'But I guess you'd better get back to the office before the fearsome Miss Burnett notices how long you've been away.'

'I am allowed a lunch hour, darling,' he assured her, but a glance at the face of the grandfather clock in the passageway hastened his footsteps and, with a hurried promise to see her soon for dinner, he was gone.

Emma stood a moment at the open doorway after his car had disappeared from sight, unable to stifle the unsettling feeling that she shouldn't have hurried his departure as soon as he'd mentioned their marriage. It wasn't as though she didn't want to set a date, she reasoned as she made her way back to the sitting-room, but her grandmother's heart attack had thrown her life into turmoil and, what with moving into her cottage so that she was on hand to run Holberry Animal Sanctuary and suspending her own career as a graphic designer she had quite enough to think about without planning the wedding of the year!

Gazing, unseeing, at the eccentrically-furnished, dusty, but comfortable parlour, Emma wondered why Nigel was adding to the pressure. Next moment she was censuring herself for her uncharitable thought. The man loved her and wanted to marry her! Since coming into her life he had provided the sort of stability she craved after living a globetrotting existence with her unconventional parents. She would find time to plan the sort of wedding he longed for, very soon. But right now she had more pressing matters to attend to.

★　★　★

Emma rubbed the back of her neck and then gave a surreptitious stretch, trying not to disturb her neighbour at the crowded table. Snapping shut her notebook, she eased her chair back, picked up her bag and then returned the book she had been working on to its place on the shelves. Leaving Summerton reference library she congratulated herself on a good afternoon's work. She now had quite a few ideas filed away in her notebook for fundraising activities, ideas she needed to act on if she was going to save Holberry Animal Sanctuary from closure.

None of her worries must be apparent to her grandmother, she reminded herself, as she turned into the driveway which led to the small nursing home where Martha Holberry was currently recuperating and as she drew the car to a halt the door opened immediately to reveal the owner, Miriam Taylor.

Miriam's smile was welcoming as they entered the corridor where Martha's room was and, not for the first time, Emma uttered mental thanks to the doctor who had referred them here. The régime Miriam insisted on was suited to Martha's strong-willed, rather capricious nature, and, despite her protests, Emma knew her grandmother was in the best place.

'There you are. I wondered if you were going to show up today.'

Only just into her seventies, Martha Holberry's hair was only now being streaked by grey and her eyes were as dark and clear as ever as they narrowed on her granddaughter as she peeled off her jacket.

'Hi, Gran,' Emma said mischievously, knowing the casual greeting would be an irritant but in no mood to indulge her ill humour.

Miriam left hastily and then Emma pulled a chair out and sat down so that she was facing her grandmother.

'And how are you feeling?' she asked.

'The same as yesterday, bored. There's work to be done at the

sanctuary and I'm sitting here, twid-
dling my thumbs.'

'But we talked all this through with
Dr Brennan. If you came home now
you wouldn't be able to stop yourself
helping out with the animals and you
could bring on a relapse.'

'Hard work never hurt anyone!'

'Overwork can,' Emma countered,
'especially after what you've been
through.'

As though she knew she was in
danger of losing the argument, Martha
made an abrupt change of subject.

'How's that student shaping up, the
one who offered to help out throughout
the summer?'

'Jenny? Wonderfully,' Emma enthused.
'And as she's a trainee vet I feel quite
confident about leaving her in charge,
whilst I do other things.'

Like fundraising, she thought, but
wouldn't raise that subject!

'Good.' Martha sniffed. 'And I
suppose that means more time to spend
with that fiancé of yours.'

'With Nigel, yes,' Emma said, emphasising his name.

Why Martha always seemed reluctant to use his name was a mystery to her. Surely any grandmother would want their only grandchild to be well settled. But then, whom was she kidding? When had Martha ever behaved like a conventional grandmother?

'And our charges? How's Charles's abscess?'

One of their battle-scarred tom cats, who went by an unlikely royal name, was currently undergoing treatment for a wound caused by his inveterate fighting and by the time Emma had brought her grandmother up to date on his progress and answered a raft of other questions, she was visibly beginning to tire, a palish tinge to her cheeks.

'I don't think we'll continue with the chess game tonight,' she announced, 'only I have a very good book I'd like to get on with.'

Used to her grandmother's sudden, abrupt pronouncements, Emma said evenly, 'Whatever you wish, Gran.'

After reaching across to deposit a swift kiss on her cheek she rose.

'I'll see you sometime tomorrow then,' she said.

Barely acknowledging her farewell, Martha already had her nose in her book before Emma had left the room. Outside she had only walked a few steps when she came across Miriam walking towards her, carrying a heavily-laden tray. She stopped, her face creasing into a sympathetic smile.

'Hi, how did it go? Martha sure was in a spiky mood when I left you.'

'Well, her mood didn't mellow much,' Emma told her with a wry grin. 'I guess it's all down to frustration. Gran's always been so active with no thought of retirement! This enforced rest is driving her mad.'

'We do try and keep her occupied but she's so . . . '

'Difficult?' Emma supplied and when Miriam opened her mouth to protest Emma forestalled her with, 'Don't worry about diplomacy. I do know what a challenge she can be and I'm grateful for all that you do for her.'

She paused a moment, a pensive look on her face.

'But in spite of it all, I really do feel we must stick with the doctor's recommendation and not move her from here until she's properly fit.'

'I agree, but that day shouldn't be too far off. Martha's a real fighter. We'll get her back on her feet, you'll see.'

Miriam's professional judgement was very encouraging and, as Emma headed for the exit, she repeated the vow she had made earlier that whilst her grandmother's health was being nurtured she would do the same for the sanctuary by bringing it back from the brink of bankruptcy.

When she returned to the cottage, she was not surprised to see a light on in the parlour and as she entered the small passageway, called out, 'Jenny, is that you?'

A neat auburn head peered around

the open doorway.

'Hi, Emma. Just thought I'd stay on until you got back.'

'Sorry I'm so late,' Emma offered as she bustled into the parlour. 'I stayed in Summerton longer than I intended and then dropped in on Gran.'

'And how is Mrs Holberry?'

Emma's look said it all.

'Pass! I tried to improve her mood by telling her what a great asset you were, but not even that worked!'

The accolade had drawn colour up into Jenny's creamy skin. Emma could see that she had embarrassed the girl but, even so, wanted to take the opportunity to pay tribute.

'And I meant every word I said! Having someone as reliable as you to shoulder the burden has been a great help whilst Gran's been ill.'

'It's a pleasure. After I've taken my finals next year I'm hoping to work in a sanctuary in a developing country, so this is great experience for me.'

'What a terrific idea. See the world

and be of use at the same time,' Emma commented as she wandered across to the table to view the open log book which Jenny had just filled in. 'Everything all right, today?'

'Yes, except for Sid.'

Sid, a great Dane and one of their more troublesome charges, had been brought in by the police as a stray so they had no history for him. Arriving in poor condition it had been a long, laborious process to restore him to full health but that success had not been matched by fully attaining his trust and he co-operated with them only if, and when, it suited him.

'Gerry tried to take him out for some exercise,' Jenny elaborated further, 'but he refused to budge from his kennel.'

'Well, we might know Gerry as a kind, caring person but I'm afraid Sid just doesn't trust men,' Emma explained. 'At some time in his troubled past he's clearly been ill treated by one.'

'He seems to trust you, though. You

seem to be the only one who's been able to build up any sort of bond,' Jenny said.

'And I can also take a hint! I'll take him out for a good, long run, but it'll have to be after I've made myself some supper. I'm starving!'

By the time Emma was ready to go out, the light was beginning to fade so she slipped a slim torch into her jacket pocket. Pausing outside Sid's pen, she called his name softly and was rewarded by his appearance at the entrance to his sleeping quarters.

'There you are, you rascal,' was her affectionate greeting and when his tail began to wag vigorously she knew that she would get his co-operation.

So mellow was his mood, in fact, that she found she did not have to clip on his leash and they set off down the track which led into the local woods with him ambling by her side as though he was the most biddable pet in the world. It was a perfect moment to review what she had found out at the library and her thoughts homed in immediately on the list of charitable trusts she had compiled which might be amenable to requests for a grant. First thing tomorrow, she decided, she'd sit herself at the computer and compose a suitable letter. A smile broke involuntarily on her lips as she imagined what Martha's response would be if she ever found out about what she would term disparagingly as begging letters. The thought was followed by the fervent wish that she would never discover what methods her granddaughter had had to employ to save the shelter.

Lost in her own thoughts, Emma scarcely noticed when a rabbit appeared on the path in front of them, only alerted to the danger when Sid gave a low-throated growl. The rabbit shot off to the right of them and as Emma put out a restraining hand to clasp on Sid's collar he eluded her grasp and bounded off in the direction of his prey, her frantic call to heel not even eliciting a pause in his headlong flight. Inwardly, cursing her momentary lapse of concentration, Emma set off in pursuit.

Realising she would not be able to catch up with the fleeing dog she was just about to stop and call him once more when he disappeared from sight. Her heart hammering, she arrived at the spot which seemed to have swallowed Sid up. A quick survey told her all she needed to know. A gaping hole in a beech hedge had allowed her errant charge access into the Darrington estate, which was private and jealously guarded by its owners.

Crouching down Emma called out Sid's name once more, to be greeted by silence. Releasing a heavy sigh Emma knew she had little choice but to follow and a moment later she was scrambling through the opening. The light was now fading fast and as she straightened, she slipped her hand into her pocket to bring out her torch. The thin beam of light revealed Sid's clumsy progress, flattened bracken arching away from her on her right. She set off in pursuit once more. She simply had to find Sid as soon as possible, before he had a chance to wreak havoc. The sanctuary's days really would be numbered if they got on the wrong side of the influential Darringtons.

An overground root, camouflaged by the undergrowth, snared her right foot and catapulted her forward, the torch falling from her grasp as her hands splayed out in a protective gesture. Thick foliage broke her fall but, even so, all the air seemed to have been expelled from her body and she lay a moment to catch her breath, until, that is, a large hand was hooked under her arm and a low-timbred voice grated in her ears.

'Up you get and then perhaps you can explain yourself.'

Emma found herself being hauled upwards, but pulled away in a fury as soon as she was on her feet.

'I prefer you to keep your hands to yourself!'

The sound of her voice seemed to

have surprised the stranger. She sensed uncertainty as the harsh light of his torch was dimmed and then lowered from her face.

'I'm sorry. I thought you were one of the lads we've had trouble with.'

Emma's hand crept involuntarily towards her hair, drawn back behind her ears. Did the style really make her look boyish? Next moment she was chiding herself for bothering about her appearance. This man had no right to be accosting people in the twilight, whatever his assumptions might be. But who was he? At the first sound of his intimidating tones she had assumed it was Bill Bryant, the Darringtons' bullish gamekeeper but, a covert scrutiny assured her that the man she was facing was a complete stranger, not that she could see much in the failing light but the angle he was holding his torch at allowed its powerful rays to play across strongly-defined features, full lips set in a straight line and eyes that were deepset, as dark as midnight, and staring straight at her.

'You still haven't told me who you are, and what you're doing here,' he said, his voice laced with suspicion.

She was just about to point out that neither had he when a dark shadow moved into her range of vision on her left, moving with speed towards them. It was Sid. About to call out a joyous greeting, the words quickly turned into one of warning as she realised that he was homing in on the man confronting her. His head shot round but it was too late to take evasive action as the next moment, Sid was upon him, large jaws clamping on to the sleeve of his jacket as he began to pull him down.

'Sid! No!' Emma screamed and to her relief, and amazement, Sid obeyed her instantly, for what was probably the first time in his life.

Letting go, he licked his mouth in a gesture of satisfaction and then settled himself at Emma's feet, looking quite docile.

'Are you all right?' she asked, turning horrified eyes on his victim.

'I'll live,' was the brusque reply, 'no thanks to the Hound of the Baskervilles here.'

He cast a baleful glance at Sid who had rested his large head on his outstretched paws and now looked the picture of gentleness.

'I'm so very sorry. I'm afraid Sid hasn't got very good manners. That's why I'm in here at the moment. You see, he scooted through the hedge in pursuit of a rabbit so I just had to come and get him. I'm aware it's private and I'm sorry for trespassing.'

'It's not really the best place to be at the moment. I suggest you get that unruly hound out of here right away.'

Well, she knew she was in the wrong but did he have to be so rude? About to challenge him, she was distracted, momentarily, by a shout, barely discernible to her but having an immediate impact on her interrogator.

'I'm wanted,' he said, but before turning away, he uttered one last urgent warning. 'I meant what I said just now, leave, just go.'

Then he was gone, long legs ploughing through the tall bracken at rapid speed, to be swallowed up by the darkness.

As if I'd want to hang around, anyway, Emma thought, as she clipped Sid's leash on, and why the stranger had acted in such a cryptic and high-handed manner was a mystery to her.

'You're in disgrace,' she told the dog firmly, but he merely licked her hand with his long pink tongue and, sighing, Emma retrieved her torch from where it had rolled into a thatch of bracken and then set off for home.

Once back on the main path, she allowed herself to speculate about the stranger she had just met. Had Bryant taken on a new member of staff? As they neared the sanctuary, she brushed all other questions aside. She had enough troubles to exercise her at the moment without getting drawn into fruitless conjecture about someone she would never likely see again.

2

The following morning, as Jenny was in charge of the sanctuary, Emma was able to concentrate on composing a suitable letter to send out to charitable trusts. Her task done, she walked down to the village to post them and as she set off back home found herself humming a lively tune.

Her newly-improved mood was to last only until lunchtime, however, when a fax arrived from Nigel with details of their most pressing bills. As she tried to take in the details one thing was clear — if she honoured them, as she was determined to do, her savings account would be emptied at a time when she was not bringing any new money in. She could end up as bankrupt as the sanctuary! There was, of course, her flat in Summerton and the more she thought about a sale the more tempting a prospect it became.

Next moment, her thoughts juddered to a halt, Nigel's face rising before her as she reminded herself, a little guiltily, that she really ought to consult him before making further plans. It so happened that they were having supper together that very evening.

'You want to dispose of your flat?' Nigel exclaimed where she told him over their meal. 'Are you quite mad?'

This was not the reaction she had been expecting.

'It's something I'm considering, that's all. I'm not working at the moment and paying Gran's debts will take all my savings so I've got to bring in some funds somehow.'

'A sale would take ages to go through, and you need some cash now.'

It was a reasonable point but suddenly Emma was in no mood to be reasonable.

'I really don't know why you're making so much fuss. I mean, I won't need the flat when we're married, will

I? We'll be living in your house.'

'True, but I assumed you'd let your place out.'

He reached across to take her hand.

'You must see, darling, that property prices in Summerton are rocketing right now. It would be foolish to dispose of an asset that could be so valuable to us in the future.'

He seemed to have it all worked out and, reluctantly, Emma conceded that he had a point but her cash-flow problems still needed solving and when she put this to him he came up with a surprising suggestion.

'Whilst you have the capable Jenny to help with the animals, why not do some graphic design? It needn't be a big assignment but surely one of your regular clients could help you out with something that's easy to handle.'

'It's worth a try,' Emma agreed and at this sign of acquiescence a smile broke out over Nigel's features.

'Good, then perhaps we can put the troubles of the sanctuary to one side a moment and concentrate on choosing a dessert.'

Emma made an effort to match his improving mood and by the time they were on to their coffee, relations between them were much more harmonious than when she had raised the subject of selling her flat. Later, as she travelled home by taxi she wondered if she had allowed herself to be manipulated, only to push the uncharitable thought aside as she reminded herself that Nigel really did have her best interests at heart.

In spite of her late night, Emma was up just after dawn the following morning as she wanted to check out a heavily-pregnant, stray cat who had just been brought in by a member of the public. To her delight she found four newly-born kittens in the bed provided for the mother cat.

Satisfied that all was well, Emma tip-toed away. The fresh, clear morning air was chasing away the fatigue brought on by her late night and Emma decided to surprise Jenny by cleaning out all the dog pens before she arrived. By the time she had finished, she was more than ready for a coffee and set off for Honeysuckle Cottage.

As expected, Jenny's bike was in its usual position resting against the hedge that encircled the small front garden but there was an unfamiliar car parked in the yard and as she entered the small hallway, Jenny's laugh rang out, to be matched by much deeper tones. The parlour door swung open at Emma's touch and two faces looked back at her, Jenny's, and one with deepset brown eyes which registered a surprised recognition.

'Well, if it isn't the lady with the crazy dog.'

Emma's mouth opened and closed and Jenny rushed in to break the threatened pause.

'I guess you two have already met.'

Finding her voice, Emma said, 'Rather briefly, and we weren't formally introduced.'

'Then let me put that right,' the man said. 'Rick Delayne, locum vet of this parish.'

'Emma Holberry,' Emma returned, only to see recognition dawn once more on his face.

'So you're Mrs Holberry's granddaughter?'

He flashed a brilliant smile at Jenny, who rewarded him with one of her own, before turning back to Emma.

'I've just been hearing all about you from Jenny. She can't praise you enough for the way you've kept this place going since your grandmother was hospitalised.'

The warm words brought an unexpected flush to Emma's cheeks as she attempted to make light of her actions.

'It's the least I can do. I can't let Gran down, nor all the animals we have here. And that reminds me, we now have four more, Jenny. Evelyn's given birth to four healthy-looking kittens!'

Jenny headed for the door.

'I must go and have a look!'

Pausing with her hand on the handle she cast a look back at Rick.

'Perhaps you can come and check them out when you've seen to Charles's abscess.'

'Sure.'

After this easy assurance, Jenny was gone, leaving Emma to say, with a wry smile, 'Sorry about all the excitement, only births are very rare at our sanctuary for the simple reason that most of our animals are here because they are too old to be re-homed. Usually they end their days with us.'

'And I guess Sid, your lively companion of the other evening, comes under that heading.'

She was glad he'd referred to their first meeting. She would love to know why a vet had been guarding Darrington land late at night and decided to probe further.

'I'm afraid Sid's social skills would let him down if we tried to place him in a home,' she announced solemnly, 'but he does have his good points. He's rather protective, as you saw the other night.'

'To my cost! He almost knocked me flat!'

'Only doing his job. He thought I was under some sort of threat.'

'I guess I owe you an explanation for the heavy-handed way I behaved,' Rick said, 'and as you work in animal welfare I'm sure I can rely on your discretion. I was there helping out the local badger protection society.'

Understanding now dawned on Emma.

'Of course, the Darrington sett! It's quite an ancient one, isn't it? But I thought it had been deserted.'

'A false rumour put around to mislead the badger baiters.'

'And it hasn't worked?'

'Apparently not. We had a very good tip-off to expect a visit two evenings ago. It turned out a false alarm, but we had to be on our guard.'

'And you thought I might be involved?'

It was difficult to keep the horror out of her voice.

'I was all fired up for trouble. Remember, we're dealing with some pretty unpleasant characters, and all I could see in the poor light was an unfamiliar figure who could have been anybody!'

He sounded defensive and Emma knew he was offering an apology of sorts and decided she could afford to be a little more gracious.

'Well, I was trespassing, quite unintentionally, of course, and when I have my hair pulled back it does make me look quite boyish.'

'It's charming, shows off your high cheek bones.'

To cover her confusion, she moved across to the log book lying open on the table and, as she filled in the details about Evelyn's kittens, she said, 'I'll be making a coffee when I've done this. Would you like one?'

'I'm afraid I'll have to decline as I've already had one with Jenny and I must get on. I'll take up your offer another time, though, and we can have a longer chat.'

'That will be nice,' Emma responded in what she hoped was a non-committal kind of way and then Rick Delayne was gone and Emma was left to stand and wonder a little about him.

So mystery man was simply a new vet, keen to do his bit to help the local wildlife. Rather charming, though dangerously so. From the way Jenny had been looking at him, it was clear that Rick Delayne could have a pretty devastating effect on women, and, judging by the way he had started flirting with her as soon as Jenny had left, it looked as though he wasn't too scrupulous in his dealings with them!

Her eyes fell to her ringless left hand. Whilst doing rough work in the sanctuary, she was reluctant to wear the beautiful diamond solitaire Nigel had given her but it might be wise if Rick was going to be a regular visitor.

Next moment, she was berating

herself for her juvenile thinking. She was a grown woman. Surely she could deal with a flirt without resorting to childish tricks. Dropping the pen which she had been twisting and turning in her hands, she set off for the kitchen.

Over the next few days, she was to realise the extent of Jenny's enthusiasm for their new vet as she was regaled with information about him.

'Rick's only in Summerton on a temporary basis as he's going to Kenya in the new year to work at a conservation centre.'

'That's going to be worthwhile work,' Emma remarked politely as she took a sip from her mug of tea.

They were having their afternoon break as a full complement of volunteers was in to walk the dogs so they could afford to relax a while. Encouraged by Emma's response Jenny continued.

'It does sound fascinating. Rick's already spent two summers out there and he's promised to tell me all about it tomorrow night.'

'Tomorrow night?'

'We're going out for a drink.'

Emma couldn't resist a little teasing.

'So this is what all this is leading up to, your first date with the dishy vet!'

Jenny's flush deepened.

'Oh, it's not really a date. Rick's going to give me some professional advice and I've promised to help with his accommodation problem.'

'Does he have one?'

'I should say! He's spending a fortune on hotel bills because he can't find a short-term let. Most landlords want at least six months and Rick will be off to Africa in four. As I've rented loads of places around here, I reckon I can give him some tips on what to do.'

Emma let the chatter wash over her, a germ of an idea forming and one which was to fill her thoughts the rest of the day. Rick Delayne wanted a place to stay for the next few months, she was paying a mortgage on an empty flat and Nigel had made it quite clear that he didn't want her to sell. Renting to Rick could be the perfect solution! Once Emma had come to this conclusion she couldn't wait to put the proposal to him but it was Friday morning before she saw him again.

Turning a corner into the yard she was just in time to see him throw his case on to the back seat of his car. He was about to leave!

'Rick!' she yelled out. 'Hold on a minute!'

He leaned against his car, a smile on his face as she hurried up to him.

'I wondered where you were this morning, Emma. I was just about to leave, disappointed,' he said.

'I've been moving the goats to new pasture land,' she told him. 'Anyway, I particularly wanted to speak to you about something. Jenny's told me about your accommodation problems and, as it happens, I've got a flat in Summerton lying empty at the moment and I just thought, well — '

'That I might be the perfect tenant!'

Rick finished for her.

'Possibly, if it suits,' she replied, feeling quite hopeful of success.

'Well, let's find out. I've got to fly right now but I can snatch a lunch break today if you can get into Summerton.'

'Should be able to,' Emma said, thinking rapidly.

'Good, then write the address down and I'll see you there around one.'

Emma did as she was bid with a pencil and pocket notebook he was holding out to her and then he was sliding into the driver's seat, his final words of farewell almost drowned out as he started the engine and then roared off down the driveway.

Emma was at her flat well before the time designated by Rick in order to check that everything was clean and tidy. Fortunately she'd paid a visit only a few days before to water her plants and do some dusting and, with no-one in residence, it was looking far more immaculate than it ever had when

Emma was conducting her busy life there. The ring of the doorbell had her scurrying to the door.

'Hi,' Rick said, stepping inside, seeming to fill the small passageway and Emma turned sharply and led him back into her sitting-room.

'This room doubles as a dining-room as well,' she informed him, pointing out the oak gate-legged table set against the far wall.

'It's quite charming. I love this type of conversion. The buildings have so much more character than new ones.'

'Especially one with an industrial past,' Emma agreed. 'This place served as the granary for the whole town for almost two centuries. The walls have never been plastered and I think the developers were wise to keep the bricks exposed.'

'They are beautiful in a solid kind of way.'

Rick's right hand brushed lightly against the brick wall and then he was opening the arched, metal-framed glazed doors and stepping through them, words of approval wafting back to her.

'This balcony is an unexpected bonus, Emma.'

She followed, to find him leaning against the iron railings and looking down at the busy street scene.

'When the developers took over this building there was just an opening here, out of which sacks of grain were hoisted up and down,' she explained. 'This balcony was added on during the conversion. It's south facing and I often sit out here in the summer.'

Emma gestured towards a tall, imposing building across the square.

'The building opposite is the old corn exchange and the square below is where deals were done when Summerton was the centre of the rural economy round here.'

'Now, at a guess, I'd say that the corn exchange houses swish apartments and the square's one of the more fashionable parts of town.'

'It is rather full of bistros and wine bars.'

She'd met her own fiancé in one of them soon after moving in here but, for some reason, didn't want to dwell on that now.

'As I very rarely cook, being near a range of eating places only adds to the attractions of this flat, Emma.'

He sounded as though he had already made up his mind and, indeed, only gave cursory attention to the kitchen and bedrooms when they resumed their tour.

'I love it, Emma,' he announced as they came out of the spare bedroom. 'Have you given any thought to terms?'

Now this was going to be the hard part. Emma had looked at the cost of rentals in the local paper but still wasn't sure what to ask and whilst she hesitated Rick mentioned a sum.

'Oh, I wasn't expecting that much!' she exclaimed.

He threw his head back and gave a great crack of laughter.

'Emma! Remind me to do business with you again! It's a fraction of what I'm currently spending at the hotel and it really would suit me to stay here.'

A rapid mental calculation told Emma that it would suit her finances, too!

'I agree,' she told him, her sparkling eyes signalling her pleasure at the conclusion of the deal.

'Great, then when can I move in?'

'Well, I'll have to find somewhere to store my stuff,' she said, thinking aloud. 'Honeysuckle Cottage is already bursting at the seams.'

He brushed her concerns aside.

'Oh, don't worry about moving everything out on my account. I'm travelling light at the moment.'

His head jerked in the direction of the room they had just left.

'All I need is for you to empty some drawer and wardrobe space in the spare bedroom.'

'I guess I could do that this afternoon,' Emma responded.

'In which case I could move in this evening.'

'I guess you could,' she found herself saying.

'Six-thirty suit?'

At Emma's nod of agreement he turned on his heels.

'I'll see you later then. Don't bother to show me out.'

The last words were thrown over his shoulder and then the sound of the door opening and closing marked his exit. Emma stood a moment to reflect on what she had just done. Should she have been more cautious about such an important decision, taken more time? The answer bounced straight back at her. No! Rick needed somewhere to stay and her bank account was in urgent need of a cash injection. It suited them both to act speedily. The thought acting as a spur, Emma then set off for the kitchen where she collected some bin bags to take whatever she found in the spare bedroom.

In the event, there was little to remove so Emma next expended her energy on cleaning through what was already a pretty clean flat. It was only when she was wiping over the counter tops in the kitchen for the final time that her eyes fell on the calendar attached to the side of the freezer and she noted that today's date was ringed in red. Nigel's dinner! Tonight was when Summerton's lawyers assembled for their annual get together. She was Nigel's guest, and she'd forgotten all about it! A quick glance at her watch stoked her panic. She had no time to go back to the cottage, shower, change, return to hand over the keys and be in time for her dinner date!

A moment later, the solution dawned and she let out an involuntary sigh of relief. She'd left plenty of clothes behind here when she'd moved into the cottage. She could shower and change here and fulfil both her obligations. It was another perfect solution and Emma headed for the bathroom to shower.

After washing her hair, she dried herself and then slipped into a towelling robe. Fortunately she had left a hairdryer in her bedroom and she began to dry her hair.

When a knock came on the door, she called out in automatic response and, next moment, Rick's head was peering around the half-open door.

'Thought I'd better let you know I was here. I tried the doorbell but when there was no response I just came in as the door was on the latch.'

'I didn't hear,' Emma said, holding the hairdryer up in explanation.

What must he think of her, was her next thought, about to rent the flat to him and yet showering here as though it was still her own.

'I only remembered after you'd left that I had a dinner date tonight,' was her rushed explanation, 'and it seemed easier to change here. I hope you don't mind.'

'Of course not,' the easy reply came. 'I'm early anyway.'

'Well, I'll be with you shortly.'

Taking the hint, Rick said, 'I'll start my unpacking then.'

His head disappeared, the door closed behind him and that was Emma's cue to jump to her feet. Suddenly she didn't want to spend any more time in the flat than was necessary. Pulling open her wardrobe door she realised that she would not waste time dallying over what to wear as there was only one suitable dress, a black, off-the-shoulder gown in crushed velvet with a slim-fitting skirt which ended just above the knee. Pulling it on in record time she was relieved to find that, as she had lost weight due to the physical work she had been doing at the sanctuary, it fitted her better than ever.

Dark tights retrieved from one of her drawers and black satin shoes completed the outfit and after winding a long, pearl necklace around her neck and adding some light make-up she took one last glance in the mirror and mentally declared herself ready. After scooping her discarded clothes into a laundry bag to be collected later, she picked up her handbag and was about to leave the room when she remembered that she didn't have her engagement ring on.

Kept in a wine-coloured velvet box in her handbag, it sparkled in the light as Emma clicked open the lid, taking a moment to admire its beauty before she slipped it on her finger. She knew Nigel had gone to London to buy it and hardly dared think about its cost but if she had experienced a little disappointment when he had triumphantly produced it, that they had not chosen the ring together, she had taken care not to show it.

The sitting-room was empty when she returned but there was a cheque on the table written out to her and as she slipped it into her handbag Rick's voice broke the silence.

'That's for the first month. Hope it's OK.'

She turned round to find he'd

entered from the kitchen.

'It's fine,' she told him, with a smile, but he seemed in no hurry to continue the exchange, his widened eyes taking in her appearance and his expression one of blatant admiration.

'You look stunning, Emma.'

It would be ungracious not to accept such a compliment and Emma replied with a simple, 'Thank you,' before injecting a businesslike tone into her voice as she deliberately withdrew her eyes from his.

'I've left notes in the kitchen on how to work the various appliances but you know where I am if you need any help. All I need to do now is hand over a set of keys.'

She fished in her handbag for her spare set and held it out to him. Instead of taking the keys, though, he took hold of her hand, his eyes trained on the gem sparkling on her finger.

'You're engaged! But you've never worn a ring before.'

'I tend not to wear it during the day

as I'm involved in a lot of rough work at the sanctuary,' she explained.

It wasn't any of his business, really, and why was he holding her hand?

'Well, you wouldn't want to damage such an expensive ring,' he returned, releasing her hand as he spoke.

Could she detect a waspish note? Glancing at the frank and open expression which was now on his face she assumed she must have been mistaken but, even so, felt a need to hurry her departure and, turning away from him, murmured, 'I think that's everything. I must be getting along.'

He followed her to the door and it was a strange sensation for Emma to be shown out of her own flat by a virtual stranger who would now call it home.

'I do hope you will be happy here,' were her final words but she barely took in his polite rejoinder before heading for the stairs, her footsteps hastened by a sudden desire to see Nigel and settle once more into the safe, cosy world he had created for her.

3

Emma could hardly wait to tell Nigel the news and when they were settled in the bar with a drink she announced, 'I took on board what you said the other night about not selling my flat, so I got a tenant instead!'

Nigel, who had spent the last few minutes trying to catch the eye of his senior partner at a neighbouring table, now gave her his full attention.

'Darling, that's a marvellous idea. Who?'

'A vet, Rick Delayne, who's just arrived in the area.'

Nigel's smile broadened.

'Sounds like a good choice. Tell you what, give me all the details and I'll set aside my other work tomorrow and draw up a contract for you.'

'But we've agreed it between ourselves. Rick's already moved in.'

'What? You mean you've handed your flat over to someone you hardly know without safeguarding your interests?'

'A lot of red tape wasn't necessary,' she told him stiffly. 'Rick was in desperate need of accommodation and as he's moving abroad in a few months I didn't think — '

'You didn't think at all, Emma! How do you know this man will move out when he says he will?'

'Because I know I can trust him!'

The words had flown out of her mouth and in the awkward pause that followed she realised that it was true. There was something dependable about Rick, and Nigel's reaction was doing nothing to make her think she'd acted foolishly, but clearly, he was not prepared to back down.

'Women's intuition?' he said, barely able to keep the disdain out of his voice. 'It's not much of a basis for a business deal, darling.'

Annoyance flashed across his face and she thought for a moment he was going to continue the argument when the party at the next table, which contained his senior partner, began to stir.

'Well,' he began, and from the look on his face Emma could see that realisation was just dawning that now was not the best time to have a public row with the fiancée, 'I guess what's done is done. We'll just have to hope that your judgement is proved right.'

Emma noted that the warmth in the smile he gave her did not extend to his eyes and was left with the distinct impression that he had been thoroughly irritated by her action. This troubled her, although Nigel was soon restored to good humour when he managed to secure a place opposite his senior partner when they sat down for dinner.

Facing the wife of the senior partner, Emma found her to be a lively, interesting woman and the evening passed much more pleasantly than Emma had dared to hope after its inauspicious beginning. Immersed as he was in talking shop, she had little contact with Nigel for the rest of the night, and the disloyal thought passed through her mind that it was perhaps just as well after their tense exchange.

The evening of the dinner was followed by several days of silence in which Nigel did not call and Emma made a resolution not to be the first one to make contact. Instead she took the opportunity to spend more time with her grandmother.

'You and that fiancé of yours had some sort of row, then?' was Martha's abrupt inquiry as she set out the board for their game of chess.

'No, Gran,' was Emma's reply. 'Can't I come and visit you without being accused of neglecting Nigel?'

'Strikes me that he's neglecting you,' was Martha's reply. 'He usually takes you out in the evening. That's why you visit during the day.'

'We don't go out together every evening, Gran. Nigel often has work to catch up with and he's particularly busy at the moment.'

Martha gave a sniff.

'If you say so, dear, only don't let disagreements fester. I mean, what sort of a marriage will you have if you can't talk through differences?'

Martha's words hit home, echoing in her mind as she drove back that night, an uncomfortable realisation taking hold that she, as well as Nigel, was behaving in a juvenile way.

I'll contact him first thing tomorrow, was her last thought as she fell asleep, and attempt to end this stand-off between us.

Oversleeping next morning meant that she needed some strong coffee before she could act on her resolution and she was just pouring herself a full mug when there was a knock at the door. Emma had a welcome surprise when she was faced with a young man holding out a basket of roses.

'Miss Holberry?'

At Emma's delighted nod he handed over the basket.

'For you.'

He left, leaving Emma to carry her gift into the parlour. Of course there was no real mystery as to who the sender was and when Emma retrieved the gold-edged card nestling amongst the stalks there was just one word, **Sorry**, in Nigel's distinctive handwriting. Dear Nigel, but he wasn't the only one who needed to apologise.

'Phew! Impressive flowers!'

The words wrenched her out of her reverie and her baleful glance fell on Rick as he stepped into the room.

'Hope you don't mind me coming in but the front door was wide open.'

'I must have left it open when I brought the flowers in,' was her abstracted response.

That brought Rick's attention back to her gift.

'Had a row with the boyfriend?'

'No!'

She pointedly turned her back on him to place the basket on the table. First Gran's and then Rick's unwanted comments — couldn't people respect her privacy a little?

That appeared to be Rick's conclusion, too.

'Sorry, I should learn to mind my own business.'

The smile was disarming and Emma found herself matching it with one of her own. Then, signalling a switch of subjects, she asked, 'I hope you're finding the flat comfortable.'

'I have never been so pleased with anywhere in my life. You don't know how relieved I am to be out of a hotel and into a real home.'

Emma sensed real enthusiasm and was just about to respond when Jenny's breezy greeting preceded her into the room.

'Will this be your last visit to Charles?' she asked Rick.

'Hope so,' the nonchalant reply came. 'If everything's clean under the dressing we can sign the rascal off.'

I daresay Rick will find another reason to visit, at least whilst Jenny's here, was Emma's thought as they left together. Then she pulled her mind back to her own romance. She'd call Nigel, never mind the strictures about not interrupting him at work, and thank him. She stabbed out the number of his extension and when the voice of Sarah Burnett, his efficient secretary, came on the line, she said, 'This is Emma Holberry here, Nigel's fiancée. I'd like to speak to him, please.'

'Good morning, Miss Holberry. I'm afraid Mr Hamilton is with a client. I'll tell him you've called and I'm sure he'll get back to you when he's free.'

A click cut off Emma's reply and she was left feeling rather nettled at her abrupt dismissal. Time spent with Evelyn's delightful kittens restored her to her customary good humour, however, so much so that, when one of the volunteers informed her that she had taken a call from Nigel for them to meet at their favourite bar that evening it didn't worry her that he hadn't waited for her to come to the phone. She just resolved to dress in an outfit she knew he liked and do her very best to thaw the ice.

She knew she had made a good start when she saw the look on his face as she approached.

'Darling, you look stunning.'

'Now that sort of observation is guaranteed to get the evening off to a good start,' she said smilingly as she sat beside him.

A crestfallen look appeared on his face.

'Unlike the other evening when I behaved like a complete heel. This last week has been a complete nightmare. Please say you forgive me.'

'Of course I do, and I need to apologise, too, for not making contact sooner. Do you know, it was Gran who brought me out of my sulk, by reminding me that couples need to talk through disagreements.'

'Really? Well, as this tenancy agreement of yours is a done deal, I don't suppose we'll be quarrelling about it in the future.'

That was not quite what she had meant but she let it pass, and not wanting to spoil the moment, Emma sipped from the drink Nigel had ready for her, thanked him for the exquisite flowers and then brought him up to date with affairs at the sanctuary.

'With Rick's cheque in the bank I feel able to pay some more of our bills. It'll certainly help to relieve the pressure.'

'Oh, put that money away, darling. Send the invoices to me tomorrow.'

Emma was unable to mask her surprise.

'Are you sure?'

Immediately the words were out, she regretted her ungracious response, but Nigel had always been so ambivalent about the sanctuary, and now he was offering to subsidise it from his own pocket! A rueful smile crossed his face.

'I'm perfectly willing to share the burden, darling. I said that as soon as we realised how deep the crisis was.'

That was true, but since then relations between them had been in a state of flux and this was the first tangible sign that Nigel was now on her side in her battle to save the sanctuary. She leaned towards him and deposited a lingering kiss on his lips.

'My way of saying thank you,' she told him as she drew away.

'A method which has my full approval!'

He inched forward as though to repeat the exercise just as a voice rose high above the surrounding chatter.

'Emma! Nigel! How lovely to see you both.'

The friendly tones belonged to Jenny and as she squeezed into a seat beside them the words continued to flow.

'Phew, it's crowded in here, isn't it? I told Rick it would be but he was delayed at work so we had to meet close to his flat.'

Then Rick appeared, carrying two glasses carefully as he negotiated the crowd surrounding the bar.

'Quite a scrum,' he noted cheerfully as he set down the drinks and then sat down on the stool which Jenny had managed to pull up.

'Well, it is one of the premier places around here,' Nigel said. 'I always get here early so that Emma and I can have a comfortable seat.'

Slightly embarrassed by this smug-sounding comment, Emma gave her fiancé a surreptitious glance and was not reassured by the look of complacency on his face. If Nigel carried on in this vein he would give Rick the impression she was engaged to a stuffed shirt, and that was the last thing she wanted. She broke into the conversation.

'But I haven't introduced you two! Nigel, this is Rick Delayne, our new vet. Rick, this is Nigel Hamilton.'

'Pleased to meet you, Rick.'

The handshake between the two men was perfunctory and then Nigel added, 'I gather you're Emma's new tenant.'

'Indeed. She liberated me from an

uncomfortable, overpriced hotel.'

Emma smiled and continued in the same light tone.

'Glad to be of assistance, but the timing was pretty good from my point of view as well.'

'I'm sure it's all very convenient,' Nigel put in, 'but I believe you won't be there very long. Aren't you going abroad shortly?'

'In the new year, yes. I'm taking up a posting with a conservation charity in Kenya.'

'A charity?' Nigel's brows arched. 'That won't make your fortune, eh?'

'It's not meant to. The experience of living under the African sun and working with an extraordinary range of wildlife will be reward enough.'

He sounded defensive and Jenny opened her mouth as though to come to his aid but it was Emma who spoke first.

'What Rick will be doing is pretty much what Gran is doing at the sanctuary, putting the animals before herself. If you decide on a life in animal welfare that's usually what happens.'

'I know, darling,' Nigel said, patting her hand. 'It's a saintly life and I'm full of admiration for you all.' In an aside to Jenny he added, in mock plaintive tones, 'Working in the shark-infested world of the law, naturally, I wouldn't know anything about higher motives.'

They all laughed and suddenly the awkwardness which had threatened the conversation seemed to melt away. Jenny began to entertain them with tales of some of the more colourful lectures at the veterinary college she attended, Nigel matched her with anecdotes about his own student days but, for her own part, Emma found herself content to listen. When Jenny engaged Nigel in discussion over a dispute she was having with a noisy neighbour, however, she found herself the focus of Rick's attention.

'You're quiet, Emma,' he said softly.

She gave a heartfelt sigh.

'Enjoyably so. It's nice to sit and

relax and forget for once the, well . . . '

'Financial crisis at the shelter?'

Her eyes were drawn to his face.

'I suppose it's common knowledge that we're on the brink of a disaster.'

'Not at all. It was Jenny who let it slip. I hope you don't mind.'

'That's all right. I know you're on our side,' she told him, and picked up her drink, gazing down at it abstractedly.

'Emma, I don't want to raise any false hopes but I have a contact who just might be able to help you.'

'Tell me more!'

'Deborah Beaufoy was a client of mine for a number of years and we forged a pretty good relationship. She has a passionate interest in animal welfare and was instrumental in setting up various initiatives where I used to work. Your sanctuary might well be the sort of project she would support.'

'Could I speak with this lady? It'll need to be as soon as possible.'

He held up both hands as though to

stem the enthusiastic flow.

'I'm sure a meeting can be arranged, but I need to speak to Deborah first. How about if I call her and then get back to you?'

'That would be fine.'

It would be absolutely wonderful, Emma repeated to herself with added emphasis. Rick's friend might be just the miracle they needed right now! Shortly afterwards, Jenny announced that she and Rick had a table booked for dinner and they left, leaving Emma and Nigel alone once more.

'Lovely girl, Jenny,' Nigel remarked, breaking the silence. 'Goodness knows what she sees in that new guy of hers.'

'Rick? He's always seemed perfectly charming to me.'

'The chap's far too well pleased with himself, and I don't think he quite returns Jenny's adulation. He spent most of his time looking at you.'

Emma's response was immediate and a touch indignant.

'That's simply not true. Really, Nigel,

it's not like you to be jealous.'

That was certainly true. Nigel had always seemed completely sure of her, even to the point of irritation at times.

'I'm not jealous,' he said. 'I'm just stating what I saw, that's all.'

An uneasy silence threatened as Emma digested his words. Really, this evening, like so many others recently, promised to end up as a stand-off between them. What was happening? Was it the strain she was under trying to keep the sanctuary afloat which was causing her to overreact all the time?

Her troubled thoughts must have shown on her face for, next moment, Nigel was reaching for her hand and giving it a tight squeeze.

'Sorry, darling, if I sounded rather petulant just now. I trust you implicitly, you know that, and I can't blame any man for looking at you when I can barely tear my own eyes away.'

That was quite something coming from Nigel and Emma signalled her pleasure with a smile that lit up her face. Soon after, they left to take a stroll and enjoy the fine evening. With her arm through Nigel's, Emma found herself letting his chatter wash over her as her thoughts returned to what he had said earlier about Rick's reaction to her. Of course he was mistaken. Men in love could often be insecure, misinterpreting this type of thing. Conveniently ignoring the fact that insecure was not a label to be attached to Nigel, Emma concluded that must be the case and put it from her mind.

4

Emma did not forget Rick's promise to speak to Deborah Beaufoy, and an anxious few days followed before she answered her mobile one morning to find Rick on the line.

'Hi, Rick here. I spoke to Deborah last night and she would really like to meet you.'

'That's fantastic! Shall I call her and arrange something?'

'That's all been done. If it's OK with you I've arranged for us to go over on Sunday.'

'Well, I am free, that'll be lovely.'

'Good, it's in Surrey, about an hour's drive. I'll pick you up at eleven.'

She answered in the affirmative and as she replaced the receiver couldn't help thinking that it was opportune that Nigel would be out of town at the weekend visiting his parents. In his present mood he was quite likely to misinterpret their innocent venture and make a fuss, so when he asked about her plans for the weekend she just said she had a meeting pencilled in on Sunday with a potential donor and he showed no further curiosity. Not a lie, she told herself defensively, just a little lacking in detail.

On Sunday morning she found herself waiting Rick's arrival with a mixture of hope and apprehension. He appeared quite untroubled by the task ahead, dressed in a crisp white shirt with short sleeves which showed off muscular, tanned arms, and denims. He had the carefree air of a man intent on enjoying some rare time off. Emma herself, keen to make a good impression, had dressed in care in a crease-free parchment-coloured suit. She eyed Rick's casual appearance doubtfully.

'Do I look a little too formal, as though I'm about to open the village fête? Only with Deborah living in such grand circumstances I thought I'd better dress smartly.'

'Deborah judges people by much sounder criteria than outward show, a rare commodity in these image-conscious days. Just be yourself, Emma, that's all that's needed, although,' he added, 'I doubt if you'll need the jacket on as it's scorching outside.'

It was, indeed, much hotter than Emma had realised and when she had discarded her jacket, she felt her appearance to be a little less prim.

They had been driving for some time in a companionable silence when Rick announced a surprising change of plan.

'I'm afraid Deborah can't see us until this afternoon now, something's cropped up, so I thought we'd stop for lunch at Appleby, a pretty little village not far from her place and then head off for our appointment from there.'

He seemed to have it all worked out so Emma murmured her approval and then turned her attention once more to the passing countryside. It was pleasant scenery, and when they drew into the centre of Appleby her enthusiasm was unfeigned when she cried out, 'What a delightful place.'

'Picture postcard,' Rick agreed as he negotiated his car into the one remaining space in the tiny street which passed for the main thoroughfare.

Cottages directly fronting the street and festooned with window boxes and colourful hanging baskets stood cheek by jowl with a variety of shops, their striped awnings drawn up and neat lettering proudly proclaiming their specialities above their shop fronts.

'Appleby still manages to retain a real village feel in spite of having its fair share of commuters,' Rick remarked as Emma joined him on the pavement, 'not to mention one of the best pubs in the area.'

Emma had to agree with his assessment of the White Swan when they stepped inside, its low-ceilinged rooms, exposed beams darkened with age and roughly plastered walls providing the perfect backdrop for a traditional hostelry. At Rick's suggestion they took their drinks outside and settled at a table beneath a huge parasol which threw a protective shade over them. They were on a narrow terrace cut out of a grassy slope which ran down to the river's edge. They watched in silence as a pair of swans made their stately progress down river. It was Rick who spoke first.

'Tell me, have you always worked at the sanctuary with your grandmother?'

'Strictly speaking I don't work at the shelter all. I just stepped in to run things when Gran got sick. She doesn't have anyone else, as my parents live in Spain.'

She could see she'd surprised him.

'What's the day job, so to speak? You seem to have such a way with animals it's difficult to imagine you in another sphere.'

'Well, I'm a graphic designer, working on a freelance basis.'

He seemed intrigued.

'And have you always been self-employed?'

'No. After art college, I taught for a few years, started taking on commissions then a couple of years ago threw up my job to go freelance.'

It had been a gamble which had just about paid off but if this current hiatus in her career continued for too long she might just have to consider another teaching job, and lose all the perks and freedoms of a self-employed life. Lost in her disquieting thoughts it was a moment or two before Rick's words registered.

'You think there might be some work for me?' she repeated, almost incredulous as she realised what he had been saying.

'I'm not sure. I'm just saying that one of the vet practices I go to, Green's on the High Street, is putting out a glossy new brochure and they've just rejected what their designer has offered. Too unimaginative, apparently, so there might be an opening there.'

'Right, thanks for the tip. I'll get on to them.'

Rick picked up two menus from the table and handed one over.

'They do delicious food here. Would you like to choose something?'

Emma nodded happily that she would but, in deference to the heat, chose a relatively light meal and as she ate, she was happy just to listen as Rick spoke about his forthcoming trip to Africa.

'I did a reconnoitre about six months ago, and was quite bowled over,' he enthused. 'The sheer scale of the place! Immense skies, with such sunsets, and the horizon seems to stretch for ever. As for the wildlife . . . '

When he started describing Nairobi and forgot the name of the site he was talking about, Emma supplied the answer. He looked at her in surprise.

'It's time to come clean,' she said and laughed. 'You see, I spent a good deal of my childhood in Africa, plus a lot of other places around the globe. Dad was a mining engineer, willing to go anywhere the prospects were good, and Mum shared his happy-go-lucky outlook.'

Picking up on the doubtful note in her voice he prompted, 'And you?'

'I was much less happy about our footloose existence. It was difficult to make friends when I knew we weren't going to set down roots and my education was always being disrupted, so when I turned eighteen, I persuaded my parents to allow me to study art in London. Then, when I graduated I came to Summerton to be near Gran, the only relative I have in the country. And it was the best decision I ever made! I found the home I'd always wanted, the stability I'd always craved.'

'And the man you're going to marry?'

'That, too.' Emma smiled brightly. 'The icing on the cake.'

There was a pause and then Rick said, 'It strikes me that our lives have taken opposite turns. You sought a safe, rooted existence in response to an unsettled childhood and I'm now wanting to leave all that behind in search of the excitement of the unknown.'

What he said was absolutely true. They wanted quite different things.

'I guess it wouldn't do for us all to be the same.'

As soon as the words left her mouth she regretted them. They sounded so lame! He seemed to think so, too. His eyes were still fixed on the river scene and he was clearly in no hurry to reply. When his words came they were a surprise.

'I guess life doesn't come much safer than being the wife of a country solicitor.'

'You make it sound as though I've picked a pension plan instead of a husband,' Emma protested. 'I'll be continuing with my career after we're married, not sitting around sharpening Nigel's pencils. He has quite a formidable secretary to do that, not that it's any of your business, of course,' she finished crossly.

'Ouch!'

Grimacing in mock pain, Rick held up one hand as though to ward off further blows.

'Sorry if I was a bit too personal just then, but if I promise to behave will you allow me to leave in one piece?'

The penitent look on his face was so ridiculous that Emma burst out laughing and the awkwardness of the moment passed. Not long afterwards they set off and found their destination only a short drive from the village. Divided from the road by only a short driveway the house's neat proportions and pale-coloured stone had all the hallmarks of an ecclesiastical house and as they parked in front of the set of semi-circular steps which led to the white, panelled door, Rick confirmed that it once had been a rectory.

The door was open even before they had climbed out of the car and they were greeted by a tall woman with strong, tanned features, expertly-cut grey hair, dark eyes that seemed to look right through you and, as Emma found when she accepted the outstretched hand, a vigorous handshake. Rick was received much less formally with a kiss on both cheeks and then she was leading them out of the hallway.

'Come through to the conservatory and I'll have tea served,' she said.

The conservatory was a modern addition, in Victorian style, and Emma was relieved to find that not only were its double doors open to allow the air in but that all the blinds on its glass ceiling were in place, shading them from the afternoon sun. Small cakes were set out on a cake stand on a wickerwork table in the centre of the room.

'Do take a seat, Emma,' Deborah Beaufoy said. 'Mrs Brown will be along shortly with the crockery and the tea.'

The warm tones and the easy use of her first name put Emma at her ease and by the time a pleasant-faced woman arrived to lay out delicate china, with a large matching tea-pot, they had exchanged pleasantries about their journey and Emma was beginning to think that the task of gaining Deborah's support might not be quite so daunting after all.

'Mrs Brown does all her own baking,' Deborah said, after handing over their teas, 'so eat as much as you like, or she would be quite offended.'

'We can't have that,' Emma said with a smile as she reached out.

'It's nice to see a young woman with a good appetite,' Deborah noted. 'So many of them nowadays seem to be on perpetual diets.'

'It's the opposite for me,' Emma said. 'Since I started working in the sanctuary I've been perpetually hungry.'

Her mention of the sanctuary seemed to be the cue for Deborah to switch to business matters and she pushed her empty plate away from her, her tone noticeably brisker when she spoke.

'When Rick spoke to me about your predicament I was naturally interested but even more so when I realised I'd met your grandmother.'

Rick and Emma exchanged surprised glances as Deborah continued.

'We were at a conference organised by a major charity for anyone involved in animal rescue and hit it off right away. I'm very sorry to hear she's been unwell, Emma. I do hope she is on the road to recovery.'

When Emma confirmed that she was Deborah went on.

'Even though I spent only a short time with Martha, her commitment to the animals in her care was clear, as was her independent spirit. I gather she doesn't know about this meeting today.'

'I'm afraid not,' Emma confirmed. 'For someone who runs a charity she is remarkably hostile about asking anyone for help.'

'Then how on earth do you survive?'

'We have a band of loyal volunteers and regular donors, a list which has hardly been added to since Gran opened the shelter, but the bulk of the financing comes from Gran's invest-ments, not doing too well recently.'

'And are the donations from your regular supporters gift-aided so that you can claim tax back?'

Emma had to admit that they were not.

'Their records are not even compu-terised,' she admitted. 'I gave my old computer to the shelter but Gran refuses to use it.'

It seemed almost disloyal to talk about her grandmother like this but if Deborah was to help them she needed to know what she was getting into. The same thought seemed to be occurring to her, the look on her face pensive. At last she spoke.

'I'd like to visit you at the sanctuary, Emma, to see if I can offer some help and, if that is the case, then I really must speak to Martha before matters proceed any further. Is that acceptable to you?'

'Yes, of course. We'd be delighted to see you at the sanctuary.'

'Good, then I'll look in my diary and call you soon.'

Her gaze now switched to her companion.

'I hope our shop talk hasn't been too boring for you, Rick.'

He gave her an easy smile.

'Not at all. That's why we came, after all.'

'Well, now that we've come to some sort of resolution let's not waste any more of this beautiful day. I've just had a new pond built,' she explained, 'adjacent to my wildlife garden. Let's see if you think I've done enough to bring the frogs and toads in.'

The query was addressed to Rick and she drew her arm through his as she ushered them through the open doors into the garden. They spent a good hour walking around Deborah's beautiful garden, expressing their delight at what she had created there and discussing her future plans. All too soon, it seemed to Emma, Rick was looking at his watch and with a show of reluctance which seemed unfeigned, saying that they had to leave.

They had only been in the car a few minutes when she declared, 'Rick, I really like your friend.'

'I hoped you two might hit it off. Deborah could be of enormous help to the sanctuary if things work out.'

'You mean if Gran co-operates,' she interpreted for him.

'Yes,' he agreed smilingly.

They lapsed into silence and after an eventful, sunfilled day, Emma felt rather languorous. Her eyelids began to droop and she allowed herself to give into the sleepiness trying to claim her.

'Emma.'

The softly-spoken name had nothing to do with her, was her first thought, but another insistent repetition brought a reluctant wakefulness, and her eyes opened to find Rick's face only a few inches from hers. The eyes, which she had always thought so dark, she could now see were flecked with tiny amber lights and in their revealing depths was a message she was unable, or unwilling, to decipher.

She pulled herself up abruptly and he withdrew, saying, 'You looked so peaceful it seemed a shame to wake you, but we're home.'

Emma thanked him for everything and he showed no signs of re-starting the engine and leaving, she wondered if he was expecting her to invite him into the cottage for refreshments. As she was pondering what to do the ring of a phone broke the silence.

'That must be Nigel. He'd expect me to be home at this hour.'

She scrambled out, threw a hasty farewell to Nick over her shoulder as she tore up the path and managed to open the door and reach the phone before it stopped ringing. In the event it was Jenny, asking if she could bring a friend the following day to help out. Expressing her approval it occurred to her that extra help had come at a most opportune moment as she was intend-ing to speak to Green's veterinary practice in the morning and might well have to go into Summerton.

Her optimism proved correct. The chief vet offered to speak with her during his lunch hour and midday found her in conference with him as he tried to explain what he wanted of his new advertising material. She was able to help clarify his thinking until she had a brief she could work on.

'I'll get back to you soon, with some suggestions,' she promised as she prepared to go.

'I'll be most grateful,' Mr Mulgrew said, as he escorted her out.

Emma got to work as soon as she returned to the cottage and as she sat in front of her computer she felt a deep sense of satisfaction that, once more, she was practising her profession. Much as she loved working with the animals, her graphic design career was what she had built up through her own efforts, and it felt good to be exercising her skills again.

So engrossed was she in her task that

she failed to take note of the time and it was only when Jenny peered round the half-open door of her room and asked if she wanted a cuppa that Emma gave a yell.

'Is that the time? I was supposed to be at Gran's half an hour ago.'

'Guess you won't be wanting a drink after all,' Jenny said.

'No, thanks, love,' she confirmed, breathlessly. 'I shouldn't be too long but if I'm not back by the time you leave just make everything secure.'

Used to the routine, Jenny just nodded and then Emma was heading for her car. Thankfully, by the time she was parking in front of the entrance to the nursing home she was not as late as she had feared. Even so, as she walked into Martha's room she had her apology ready, only to find it evaporating on her lips as she took in her grandmother's face.

'Gran, what on earth's the matter? I know I'm a bit late, but — '

'What's that got to do with anything?'

She brandished a letter she had been clutching in her hand.

'Those Darringtons think they only have to snap their fingers and we'll all stand to attention.'

Now thoroughly alarmed, Emma cried out, 'But, what have they done?'

'Made me an offer for my house and land. They want to buy us out.'

5

It took a few seconds for Martha's words to sink in and then Emma was reaching out for the letter. Her eyes scanned it and widened when she got to the sum offered. She returned her gaze to her grandmother.

'Why would the Darringtons want to buy us out when they already have so much land of their own?'

'That's no concern of mine, Emma. Probably they just don't want us as neighbours. Well, they won't get rid of me that easily.'

She pulled the letter from Emma's hand, screwed it up, and then threw it into the waste-paper basket.

'But aren't you even going to reply?'

'Why should I? I didn't ask to be pestered.'

'But, Gran, you should at least

consider this offer. You'd have enough money to start afresh somewhere else.'

'There's nothing wrong with the facilities we have now, Emma, and I never thought I'd see the day when my own flesh and blood would side with the snooty Darringtons against me.'

Emma's eyes rose heavenward as a sigh escaped her lips.

'OK, have it your own way, but you should put your refusal in writing.'

'I'll think about it,' was the mumbled reply but Emma had little doubt that the crumpled-up letter would remain unanswered.

Nigel's reaction that evening when she told him about the offer to buy was instantaneous.

'But that's wonderful, darling. All your debts will be paid and there'll be masses of money left over to start up a new shelter.'

'Hold on a moment. You haven't heard about Gran's reaction yet.'

'She's going to turn it down?'

'She won't even consider it!'

'But you must get her to change her mind.'

'She won't budge, Nigel.'

'Then you must try again,' he insisted. 'You'll regret it if she misses this opportunity.'

'I'll regret it if I upset her and hinder her recuperation,' she warned him. 'That would be the worst outcome for all of us.'

As if aware that this insistence had gone too far Nigel patted her hand.

'I'm not suggesting undue pressure, darling, just that you should raise the topic again when she's in a better frame of mind.'

Somewhat mollified, Emma agreed to try.

'But I'm not optimistic about my success,' was her candid admission.

Over the next few days, however, Emma put the problem to one side as she concentrated on the design ideas she was to present at the end of the week to the chief vet at Green's. She settled on some bold, innovatory designs and on Friday morning realised that her gamble had paid off when the completion of her presentation was greeted with warm words from Mr Mulgrew and his assembled team. The commission was approved there and then and when Emma left she felt as though she was floating on a cloud of her own, only to walk straight into Rick.

'From the expression on your face, you've just received good news.'

'I've got the job!' the words bubbled to Emma's lips. 'It's the first graphic design I've been able to do in ages. I'm so excited.'

A swift look at his watch was Rick's response and then an invitation.

'Let's celebrate. Champagne's in short supply round here,' he told her with a wry smile as he took her arm, 'but there's a nice little coffee shop round the corner where we should be quite comfortable.'

It was a cosy place and, ensconced in a corner table, they were served with large cups of café latte.

'I should really be treating you,' Emma remarked, 'as it was your tip-off that helped me clinch the deal.'

'I don't think we'll quibble about a cup of coffee,' he returned. 'Let's just enjoy five minutes' peace and quiet out of our busy schedules.'

The conversation turned to general topics and then Rick was asking if she'd heard anything from Deborah.

'Indeed, I have. She's coming over on Wednesday to look around and then we'll take it from there. If she does want to help us then I guess I'll need to arrange a meeting between her and Gran.'

'And you think that'll be a problem?'

'Not really. It's just that Gran's been put into rather a bad mood.'

Suddenly she found herself telling him about the Darrington offer.

'I tried to get her to see the advantages it could offer but Gran chose to see it as an attempt by the Darringtons to insult her. She wouldn't listen to a word I said.'

Rick looked at her reflectively in the pause that followed and then said, 'I daresay that was just a defence mechanism. The thought of uprooting herself from her home of many years was probably so scary that she refused to even consider it.'

Emma was not to be mollified.

'You're right to point out the ill effects a move could have on Gran. The letter from the Darringtons can remain where Gran filed it, in the bin.'

They laughed and the conversation moved on to other matters.

When Wednesday dawned, she and Jenny awaited Deborah's arrival.

'If Mrs Beaufoy likes us all our worries might be over,' Jenny announced as they were filling the bowls with cat food in the cattery.

'That might be a touch optimistic,' Emma told her with a smile, 'but her help certainly could ease the immediate crisis.'

Just then, they heard the car through the open windows. Emma wiped her hands on a towel and then hurried out into the sunshine. As soon as the words of welcome left her lips, however, and were matched by Deborah, her nerves seemed to melt away and the easy rapport which they had established on their first meeting was back.

Afterwards, Emma was to conclude that taking Deborah into the cattery first was a masterstroke as she was immediately smitten by Evelyn's offspring. Evelyn, who had turned out to be a very laid-back mother, stretched out to enjoy Emma's attentions whilst each of her tiny kittens were cradled in turn by Deborah.

When they moved on to the kennels, Emma found herself apologising for the shabbiness of the structures but Deborah brushed her words aside.

'The buildings have seen better days but the runs are spotlessly clean, the dogs have comfortable beds and I can see from their reaction to us that they are well socialised.'

It was indeed remarkable but their

charges seemed to sense that something important was afoot. Sid simply sat and looked at them with his big brown eyes as though he always behaved in such a sensible fashion and Toby, a Jack Russell who had the unfortunate habit of continually chasing his tail, was curled up in his basket, a look of contentment on his face.

By the time the tour was over and Emma was taking Deborah inside for lunch, she was heaving an inward sigh of relief that everything had gone off well and this was confirmed when Deborah offered her congratulations.

'You and your grandmother do a really good job here, Emma, and I don't intend to keep you in suspense. I would like to help you out.'

'Deborah, that's marvellous!'

Deborah leaned back in her chair, her lunch temporarily forgotten.

'In fact I'd like to do a little more than help out with a donation. I've time on my hands, quite a bit of experience with fundraising, and I think I could help to widen your support base.'

'But that's even better! We'd love you to become part of the team, as long as, well . . . '

It was Deborah who supplied the missing words.

'As long as Martha agrees?' she said and when Emma gave a nod of affirmation she continued with, 'I meant what I said at my house. I would like to speak to Martha. I think I can talk her round.'

'Do you know, Deborah, I think you might be right!' Emma said.

They resumed eating in a companionable silence but despite her outward composure, Emma's mind was in a fever of excitement. So much could be achieved if Deborah was brought on board! Please let it happen, was her fervent wish.

Eager to tell Nigel of the day's events, they had barely settled into their seats in the corner of the country pub where they were to have dinner when the words spilled from her lips. His reaction surprised her.

'I'm sure this all sounds wonderful, as long as Martha approves, that is, but it'll hardly give you the financial security you need, will it? Only a profitable sale will do that. Have you managed to talk to Martha again about the Darrington offer?'

Thoroughly put out by the way he had received her news she felt under no obligation to be diplomatic.

'No, and I don't intend to.'

'But you promised.'

'Well, I've had a re-think and decided Gran's health is too fragile to cope with the upheaval a move would bring.'

'It's too fragile to cope with all the cares of a shelter blighted with financial insecurity. The situation's already brought on one heart attack. Worse could follow if nothing's done to lift the burden.'

What he said had some truth in it but Emma found herself resenting what could be seen as scare tactics to win an argument and she put up an immediate defence.

'I'm doing everything I can to help Gran but the last thing she needs is added stress, from any quarter.'

'I care only for your interests, Emma, and as I'm going to be part of the family soon I would have hoped that my words would carry some weight.'

'Of course they do, but I just can't agree with you on this, so we'd better let the matter rest.'

He muttered something non-committal but his expression remained thunderous and, not for the first time recently, Emma found herself making surreptitious glances at her watch during dinner as the atmosphere remained strained between them.

The next few days found her pre-occupied with her new design commission. It was a joy to be back in front of the computer, putting flesh on the ideas she had sketched out for the team at Green's and the therapy of her return to work helped to put her in an optimistic frame of mind for the meeting she had arranged between Deborah and her grandmother.

To her surprise, Martha had been remarkably receptive to the idea of a visit from Deborah. Following Deborah's advice she had pitched the visit simply as a social one and, when the two women were settled with drinks, Emma announced that she needed to speak to Miriam about something and then left them alone.

'I do hope this ploy of Deborah's works,' she confided to Miriam as they were sipping coffee in Miriam's office.

In the nervous moments that followed, she and Miriam drank fresh cups of coffee and then a glance at the clock showed Emma that she had stayed away long enough.

'Wish me luck,' were her parting words.

The look on Deborah's face was restrained but the glance she flashed Emma spoke volumes. It was Martha who spoke first, however.

'Well, Emma, you're back at last. Whilst you've been out Deborah and I have had a good, long chat and we've come to the conclusion that it would be a very good thing if she were to help out at the shelter.'

'What a wonderful idea,' Emma approved, looking at Deborah.

'Martha thinks my skills will come in useful and I'd love to be able to contribute to the good work you're doing.'

It was a modest assessment of what Deborah would be offering them but Emma played along and by the time they left they had Martha's blessing for a whole host of changes.

'I don't know how we did it,' Emma marvelled on the way home. 'I've never known Gran to be so co-operative. Deborah, you're a miracle worker!'

A wry smile passed over Deborah's face.

'I think you over-estimate my powers of persuasion. Remember, Martha already knows and respects my work, believes she can trust me and I don't intend to let her down. Now, I need to run some ideas past you.'

She spoke of setting up a supporter data base, introducing an animal sponsorship scheme, and seeking publicity through the local media but it was her final suggestion which had Emma's ears pricking up.

'And to celebrate a new beginning for Holberry Animal Sanctuary, I think we should stage a high-profile event, a ball.'

'A ball! But where? And who would organise it?'

'Oh, I'd do that,' Deborah said as though organising balls was an everyday occurrence. 'A friend of mine has a very suitable house where it could be held and I know quite a few people who could be persuaded to buy an expensively-priced ticket in aid of a good cause. It can't fail, Emma.'

Her optimism was infectious and as Emma gave a welcome to the proposal, the thought came to her that, with

Deborah on board, life at Holberry Animal Sanctuary would never be quite the same again.

Deborah made her effect felt the very next day. A makeshift office had been created by Martha out of an old scullery and had stayed pretty makeshift, so Deborah set about putting it into better order. The computer, which had been gathering dust, was put to work and in no time the shelter's supporters were on a data base and Deborah had begun work on a newsletter to send out to them.

Over the next week she firmed up her plans for a fundraising ball and, after some frantic phoning around, was able to announce to Emma that she had booked Netherton Hall, a large country house, for the end of the month.

'Teddy Netherton was at school with my late husband so he was only too happy to oblige, and the venue should secure us the favours of some well-heeled guests. Now, who can cater for us, for little or no expense?'

She frowned at her open filofax as though it should supply the answer and then a forefinger descended on a name.

'Marie Tallier. She adores publicity and if I can promise her the right kind she'll do the buffet at cost.'

Realising she was redundant, Emma tiptoed out of the office as Deborah began to stab out a number on the phone. Entering the parlour she was surprised to find Rick there, just about to pour a mug of coffee from the machine on the table. He acknowledged her greeting with a smile and then asked, 'And how are you getting on with Deborah?'

'Wonderfully, but it's a little like inviting a whirlwind to stay and I'm finding it difficult to keep up.'

'That's what Jenny says.'

This reminder of his girlfriend prompted her to say, 'She's not in today, by the way, if you're hoping to see her.'

'I know that but I've come to see another beautiful female.' There was suppressed amusement in his dark eyes but Emma managed to maintain a neutral expression until he said, 'Of course, I'm referring to Evelyn.'

'I know that,' Emma returned smoothly. 'If you care to bring your coffee I'll walk down with you to the cattery.'

Evelyn was currently causing concern as she had been observed sneezing the day before. She had been separated from her kittens for fear of passing on an infection and Emma was now bottle feeding them.

'I want to avoid giving her antibiotics because they would be passed through her milk to her kittens so we would have to keep the family apart for much longer but if she develops a full-blown infection that's what we'll have to do,' Rick explained as they entered the pen.

'She hates being apart from her little ones,' Emma said as she held the cat whilst Rick examined her, 'but we've got to quarantine her until we know what's going on.'

'Quite right,' Rick murmured abstractedly, looking into Evelyn's ears.

A moment later he was looking up, a pleased expression on his face.

'There's no sign of infection here, Emma. The sneezing was probably a reaction to some dust, that's all. Just to be on the safe side, keep her under observation for another twenty-four hours then, if all's well, the kittens can be returned to her.'

They went back out into the sunshine. Emma told him about Deborah's plans for the ball, only to find that Jenny had kept him informed.

'She's really cut up that she's going to miss it.'

'Jenny won't be there?'

'No, she's to go home that weekend for a family do, a christening.'

'Well, I hope you'll still be able to come. You've done so much for us.'

'Of course I'll come.'

'The ball's not the only idea Deborah has for increasing our funds.'

She went on to list some of them and this led to an animated discussion on the best way to proceed. Later, when she was attempting to grapple with a particularly tricky part of her design brief she found her mind wandering back to Rick. He hadn't seemed too concerned about Jenny's absence. Did he have someone else in mind for his date for the night? And how would that affect Jenny? She had a trusting nature, and could hurt all too easily. Emma made a fervent wish that heartache was not in store for her friend.

★   ★   ★

Emma made no attempt to mask her displeasure.

'Nigel, what do you mean by saying you can't come to the ball with me?'

'I've just explained, darling, the date clashes with work commitments. We're going on a weekend training session. I told you about it months ago.'

That's right, he had, but it hadn't

mattered then because nothing else had been planned.

'Well, can't you explain about the changed circumstances and pull out?'

'I can't. What would the senior partners think of me?'

'But this is very important to me.'

'And this is important to me. It's a great opportunity. It is our joint future I'm thinking about, Emma.'

Feeling rather ashamed of her waspishness, Emma offered an apology.

'I'm sorry. It's just that I'm so disappointed you won't be with me.'

'Me, too, darling, but I'll make it up to you when I get back, I promise.'

With that, Emma had to be content but her heart was heavy at the thought of going to the event at Netherton Hall without her fiancé.

6

Emma looked at herself glumly in the dressing-table mirror. Why take pains with her appearance when Nigel would not be at the ball? Because plenty of the other people will be and you owe it to Deborah to present your best face to the world, she told herself. She picked up her hairbrush and began to brush her hair back from her face vigorously. After quickly putting on some light make-up she slipped into her new gown.

She couldn't help but feel a sense of satisfaction when she saw how well she looked in the blue gown, its satin sheen and the way it clung to her curves giving her a decidedly slinky appearance. It was Deborah who, on a day out in London, had persuaded her to make the bold purchase and, as she picked up her matching clutch bag and slipped into her high-heeled sandals, she hoped once more that she would not let her friend down.

An hour later, as she shook hands for the umpteenth time and beamed at another complete stranger, she felt sure that her mascara must be running in the heat generated in the crowded entrance hall but when she managed to whisper her concern to Deborah she was quickly reassured.

'You look wonderful, Emma. Quite immaculate, in fact.'

'I don't feel it. I feel quite hot and bothered.'

'Well, it doesn't show. Most of the guests have arrived now so we won't be on reception duty much longer.'

Within half an hour, the flow of guests had slowed to a trickle.

'Let's go through,' Deborah suggested, putting her arm through Emma's, 'and see what's happening.'

They slipped through double doors on their left and Emma had to stop a moment to take in the scene. Having left all the arrangements to Deborah, she had no idea what to expect, but it hadn't been anything quite on this scale. The ball was taking place in a galleried hall which had once been the heart of this manor house and its wood-panelled walls were garlanded with greenery intertwined with creamy white lily heads and silvered satin bows. The highly-polished wooden floor provided the ideal surface for dancing and couples were already taking advantage of the music provided by the live band ensconced in the gallery at the head of the hall.

'Deborah, you've worked magic. Everything looks so beautiful!'

'Well, Teddy pitched in once I'd told him what we wanted. I couldn't have got everything prepared in time without his help.'

As though her words had conjured him up, he hove into view, right hand rising automatically when he caught sight of them. He acknowledged Emma with a smile and then issued her friend with a challenge.

'I've two left feet but I'm willing to take a chance with the next waltz. As Lord of the Manor I insist on my rights. Don't you agree, Emma?'

Emma did so laughingly, shooing them both on to the dance floor. She reflected inwardly that Deborah seemed to be in for a good night with her old friend. Feeling lost she collected a glass of sparkling champagne from a tray held out by a waiter and set out to find a table where she could sit and watch. Emma had no sooner sat down than she heard a familiar voice.

'There you are. I wondered when you'd get away from your hostess duties in the entrance hall.'

It was Rick, and Emma experienced an unexpected rush of pleasure at the sound of his voice. She had never seen him in a formal dress suit before and the contrast between the white pleated silk shirt and his dark colouring seemed to add lustre to his brown eyes and newly-tamed thatch of hair. His suit fitted immaculately, and Emma was quite unable to rein in her surprise.

'You look very smart!'

He gave out a shout of laughter.

'For a change, you mean.'

He pulled up a stool and sat across from her.

'I guess you're only used to seeing me in my shabby working clothes.'

'Not at all,' Emma said, now quite embarrassed. 'I meant that you look particularly nice. Anyway,' she went on, suddenly deciding that she didn't want to stand on ceremony with Rick, 'I wouldn't have cared if you'd turned up wearing a sack, I'm just glad to see a friendly face. I mean, Deborah has worked wonders getting all these well-heeled people to come but I don't know anyone.'

The look Rick gave her was sympathetic.

'I guess it was rather tough having to come on your own tonight.'

'Not really. This ball was arranged at the last minute and Nigel had prior commitments. It couldn't be helped.'

She took a sip of her champagne, announced it to be delicious and was grateful when Rick did not pursue the subject of her fiancé's absence.

On the dance floor, Teddy and Deborah glided past.

'Teddy seems to be very fond of Deborah,' Emma said.

'I should say so. He's been trying to get her to marry him for the last couple of years. They and their late spouses were all good friends and when he was widowed himself he turned to Deborah for support. Now he'd like them to become closer still but Deborah's an independent lady and she's holding out.'

'Well, she looks very happy. Perhaps she's beginning to weaken.'

'Perhaps. But it shouldn't be left just to one hostess to show the way on the dance floor, should it?'

Older couples were deserting the dance floor as an upbeat tempo took over. She allowed him to lead her on to the dance floor but when he went to take her in his arms, she eluded his grasp to dance apart. Then, as the rhythm of the music took over, her inhibitions began to ease and she gave herself up to the moment, swaying to the lively beat.

It was the look of admiration on Rick's face which fired the adrenalin pumping through her veins as much as the music and she couldn't help but feel a glow of satisfaction that, although abandoned by her fiancé on the night, she had managed to bewitch one of the most handsome men there.

There were several fast numbers in a row, and Emma was just beginning to think of sitting one out when the tempo slowed. All around them couples were moving into each other's arms and Emma was just about to suggest they return to their table when Rick's arm snaked around her waist. She found herself pressed against his broad chest, the scent of his tangy aftershave enveloping her. Her heart seemed to be racing at breakneck speed. She couldn't dance with Rick like this, she really couldn't! As alarm gripped her, she tensed, felt Rick's grip loosen and was just about to slip out of his arms when a hand with fingernails tipped a vivid shade of lilac curled around his upper arm and drew him away from her.

The hand belonged to a tall, dark-haired woman, who now wagged her finger at him and began to speak in a rich, American drawl.

'Rick Delayne, I've been looking everywhere for you. Didn't you say you wanted to spend some time with me at this ball and have a long chat?'

When Emma looked at Rick's face for a reaction it showed nothing beyond polite interest.

'And that's just what I intend to do, Gloria, if Emma will excuse me.'

A glance in her direction elicited a nod of the head and with a promise to return soon he allowed himself to be led off by his friend. Emma remained on the dance floor for one self-conscious moment and then decided to make her way to the supper room.

The buffet laid out in one of the side rooms offered a tempting array of food to suit every taste. Her exertions on the dance floor had given her a keen appetite and she ate speedily. All too soon she was pushing her plate away and wondering, rather irritably, what to do next. Really, it was very inconsiderate of Rick to swan off with one of his glamorous friends when he knew she hardly knew anyone here.

Next moment she was telling herself off for being so pathetic. It wasn't Rick's responsibility to entertain her for the evening. Emma looked around the supper room, could not see one familiar face so decided to make her way back to the ballroom. At least there she could find herself another quiet corner and watch the dancing. As she entered through the now open double doors she almost walked straight into Teddy and Deborah.

'There you are,' Deborah exclaimed.

'We've been looking for you. Come and meet some people who are keen to know all about the sanctuary.'

There followed a dizzying round of introductions. Afterwards she was to find it difficult to disentangle one person from another, but she found the words flowing from her lips as she described the path she and her grandmother had chosen and just hoped she was able to convey some of the passion involved. Certainly Deborah seemed to think she'd succeeded.

'Well done,' she enthused after one couple took a note of Emma's phone number and promised to pay a visit. 'The Wilsons have pots of money to spend on good causes so if we get them on our side it will be a great help. Now,' she added, taking her friend's arm, and ushering her towards the dance floor, 'let's forget work for a while and get back to having some fun. Teddy's dying to dance with you.'

He whirled her around in time to the lively music and when a breathless

Emma returned him to Deborah, she explained that she needed to cool down and would seek them out later. She'd noticed an open glass door earlier and retraced her footsteps in that direction. When she slipped through it she found a well-lit flight of steps which led on to a small, stone-flagged terrace. When she went up to the parapet she found herself looking out on what would be the back garden. The air was scented with night stocks and she breathed in the perfume of the invisible flowers as a welcome breeze brushed against her cheeks.

'Here you are. I just caught a glimpse of you slipping out, otherwise I would have been running round in circles indoors.'

The tread of Rick's footsteps had preceded him and she had her smile of welcome ready for when he reached her.

'You didn't need to leave your friend on my account. I'm just fine.'

He joined her at the parapet before replying.

'Well, I'm sorry I had to go off with Gloria at all, but she's rather strong-willed, as I'm sure you gathered, and as I've been trying to pin her down for ages, I couldn't let the opportunity slip.'

'Pin her down?' Emma repeated, her expression incredulous. 'That's not a very romantic way of putting things.'

'Romance, with Gloria? Really, Emma, you've let your imagination run away with you. She's just an acquaintance.'

Aware that she had made a fool of herself, Emma's voice displayed her irritation.

'Well, she has rather an affectionate manner for a mere acquaintance.'

'Put it down to the warm manners of the deep South. The fact is I've been trying to persuade Gloria for some time to support the sanctuary financially. Tonight she finally agreed! She'll be a great asset, Emma. She's very generous towards the causes she supports.'

To her embarrassment, she found tears welling up in her eyes and, in spite of frantically trying to blink them away, Rick noticed.

'Hey, what's this? I didn't mean to upset you.'

'You didn't.'

Emma fished a tissue out of her bag and began to dab at her eyes.

'I'm just being silly and emotional, that's all. It's just that you and Deborah have been so incredibly supportive. The shelter was facing ruin before you and Deborah took some of the weight off my shoulders and now, for the first time since I realised how bad things were, I can see some hope.'

Looking down at the tissue now smudged with black, her next words were a little more prosaic.

'Now look what I've done.'

Rick took the tissue and turned her face up to face him. As he gently wiped beneath her eyes, he said, 'I'm just happy to help out, Emma. I really believe in what you're doing. Although if I were honest with myself, I guess I'd admit that my motives aren't quite as uncomplicated as I'm making out.'

She should have looked away then but his eyes seemed to be drawing her into their dark centre. His head dipped, his lips moved over hers in a gentle kiss and, for a few seconds real life seemed to be happening elsewhere. Then it intruded and Emma was pulling away, the words rattling out of her.

'That shouldn't have happened. Please, forget it did.'

He caught up with her as she reached the top of the steps.

'Let's not over react to this, Emma! It was only a brief, innocent kiss.'

It might have been brief but there had been nothing innocent about it! She looked him full in the face.

'I'm committed to someone else, Rick. That means something to me.'

'I know, and I respect that, but I don't want to lose your friendship.'

'You won't.'

She let it go at that but as she made

her way back to the ballroom to seek the reassuring company of Teddy and Deborah she couldn't help thinking that true friendship would be quite impossible from now on between her and Rick. As she smiled and chatted with her friends, they had no idea that her mind was teeming with unsettling thoughts. It wasn't Rick she blamed for what had just happened, it was herself. How could she just have stood there and allowed herself to be kissed? And it hadn't just been an affectionate kiss between friends. It had been a gesture which had told her more than she wanted to know about Rick's attraction to her. And her response had revealed that she was in serious danger of reciprocating! She comforted herself with the thought that what had happened was a timely warning, one that she should heed.

She knew that Nigel was set to arrive home early on Sunday evening and seven o'clock found her rapping on the front door of his own house in a fashionable part of town. The door swung open to reveal Nigel, a smile lighting up his features.

'Darling, what an unexpected pleasure.'

'I've really missed you.'

She planted a kiss on his face and then stepped into the hallway. He led Emma into his immaculate drawing-room and whilst Emma perched herself on the leather Chesterfield, he crossed over to the sideboard to pour out two sherries from his crystal decanter.

'Seeing you is the perfect ending to the weekend,' he enthused as he brought her drink over and then sat beside her. 'We've had a wonderful time, darling. I'm sure the senior partners see me in a new light now.'

'I'm so pleased for you,' Emma responded. 'You can tell me all about it in a minute, but first there's something I want to say.'

Now she had his full attention she took a deep breath and went on.

'I've been doing some thinking whilst

we've been apart and, with all the turmoil in my life recently, it's made me realise how important stability is to me. I need you in my life full time, Nigel. Let's set a date for our wedding!'

7

'You're getting married, but not for another year?' Martha said, giving a sniff. 'That fiancé of yours doesn't believe in rushing things, does he?'

'It's quite common to set a date a year in advance,' Emma explained. 'It'll give us more options when choosing a venue for the reception.'

'More choice for Anna Hamilton, you mean. I daresay she's planning some sort of society wedding.'

Privately Emma was already alarmed at the way Nigel's formidable mother had begun taking charge of the arrangements but she wasn't going to admit that to her grandmother.

'Naturally Anna's taking a close interest but it's Nigel and I who'll make the final decisions.'

'Mmm, if you say so,' Martha muttered almost to herself.

It was hardly a vote of confidence and Emma decided judiciously to change the subject.

'Anyway, that's not the only thing I've come to talk to you about. I've got Dr Brennan's agreement to you coming home!'

This piece of news elicited a much more positive response.

'At last! I don't know how you got the old quack to change his mind.'

Deliberately deciding to ignore Martha's provocative description of their conscientious GP Emma went on to tell her grandmother that she would be able to take her home the very next day. Arrangements were made and she was able to leave Martha in a positive frame of mind.

The following day, she drove Martha down the driveway to find Deborah, Jenny and two of their regular volunteers assembled outside the cottage as a welcoming party. Sid, improbably wearing a garland of paper flowers around his neck, ambled up to greet his mistress and then, to gales of laughter, lost interest to slump on the ground and lick one of his paws!

Inside, a buffet had been set out in the parlour and, as food and drink were passed around and Martha struck up an animated conversation with Deborah, Emma stood silently a moment and just observed. Colour was back in her grandmother's cheeks and there was a light back in her eyes.

I have done the right thing by bringing her home, she affirmed to herself and, with Deborah's help, I'll make sure that she doesn't take on too much.

There was a knock on the door, picked up by Jenny who scooted off down the hallway, only to return a moment later with Rick at her side.

'Look who's come to see you, Martha,' she said. 'Rick Delayne, our vet.'

Rick's hand was extended.

'I hope you don't think I'm intruding, Mrs Holberry, but I'd heard you were coming home today and I really wanted to meet the woman who founded this wonderful sanctuary.'

After that accolade, Rick was assured of a warm welcome and Martha drew him into a conversation about his experience with their charges whilst she'd been absent. Emma chatted with one of the volunteers, ate, and sipped mineral water but her mind seemed to be elsewhere.

She had hardly seen Rick since the night of the ball, had actively avoided him in fact, but now he was only a few feet from her and making her feel distinctly selfconscious. Why, she wasn't sure. Setting the wedding date should have ended any growing doubts about her commitment to Nigel, so why was her mood still so edgy? And what responsibility did the man currently charming her grandmother have for her current confusion?

Her inner thoughts were broken into when Martha announced that she was dying to see all the animals and they set off on an impromptu inspection. It was soon clear that Martha was impressed by the standards which had been maintained in her absence and when Deborah took her back inside to explain the changes in the office and Jenny and the two volunteers returned to their duties, Emma found herself alone with Rick.

'Thanks for coming today, Rick. Gran really appreciates it.'

'I was in the neighbourhood and it seemed a great opportunity to introduce myself. That's the truth, Emma. It wasn't just an excuse to see you. I meant what I said at the ball, friendship is all I'm seeking.'

With Jenny as his beck and call, it would be, wouldn't it?

'I know that. I hope we'll always be friends.'

She began to walk back towards the cottage, Rick still by her side.

After a moment he said, 'Jenny tells me you've decided to set a date for the wedding. This must be a happy time for you.'

'It is. We're toying with the idea of a Christmas wedding.'

'But that's only a few months off.'

'A year this Christmas,' Emma replied. 'I'm afraid it takes rather a long time to plan the sort of wedding we want.'

'Hamilton must be mad to want to wait so long.'

For a moment she thought she had misheard but when she looked at him quizzically he had the grace to look rather shamefaced.

'Sorry, just showing my ignorance. I'd no idea it took that long for two people in love to get married.'

'Well, it does,' Emma returned shortly.

They had reached Rick's car. He opened the door, then said, 'I guess I'll see you on my next visit.'

'Of course, and thanks again for coming.'

He drove off and Emma went inside to seat herself at her computer. On checking her e-mails she found one from Nigel's mother, containing the names of designers who created the most scrumptious bridal gowns. Emma stared at the screen in disbelief. How on earth could she afford to pay such sums? She decided not to reply until she had spoken to Nigel.

After pouring out her concerns his reply was unambiguous.

'I'm sure Mother would be delighted to help out, darling.'

'Oh, Nigel, I couldn't possibly let your mother buy my dress.'

'Why ever not? Mother will want you to look your best.'

Was there a subtle warning there? Don't let us down?

'I'll speak to Anna about it,' Emma said decidedly.

After a heart-to-heart with her future mother-in-law, however, she did not feel able to claim any sort of victory. She had ended up agreeing to Anna contributing to the cost of a designer gown on the understanding that it was the Hamiltons' wedding gift to her. But as Emma made her way home she wondered if she had been wise to give way. Surely she should be making it clear now, before she joined the family, that she preferred to stand on her own two feet. Otherwise what would the future hold when she was fully part of the close-knit Hamilton clan?

Thoughts about her own problems flew out of her mind when she entered the parlour and caught sight of Martha's face.

'Gran, what on earth's happened?'

Crossing the room, she crouched down beside her grandmother, her hand on Martha's hands which were twisting in her lap. There was a film of perspiration on her forehead and pallor had returned to her cheeks.

'Why didn't you tell me about our financial problems, Emma? Did you think me too old and useless to be able to cope with bad news?'

Emma slumped back on to her haunches.

'I've never thought that! I've only

ever acted in your best interests! It's true that we have been having problems but with Deborah's help we're slowly getting back on our feet. We were going to explain everything to you once we were convinced your recovery was complete. But, Gran, how do you know all this? Has Deborah said something?'

'No. That estate manager of the Darringtons has been here, Bryant. He wanted to know why I hadn't replied to their letter offering to buy me out. I told him why in no uncertain terms. He didn't enjoy my bit of straight talking one bit. I ended up having to order him out, but not before he'd told me we'd soon be crawling on our hands and knees to them because we were on the verge of bankruptcy. I felt such a fool when he went on and on about our debts and I didn't really know much about them. I'd always let Rebecca deal with that side of things, you see, then she emigrated and I was going to get it all sorted out but before I could I went into hospital. Now I just wonder what sort of a mess I left behind.'

'Gran, it's all right, really, it is. Please don't upset yourself! Look, I'll get you a nice cup of tea, then we can talk things through a bit more.'

Martha nodded in agreement and Emma went through into the kitchen. As the kettle boiled and she hastily assembled the tea things she felt such a rage against Bill Bryant that she found herself trembling. How dare he turn up unannounced to bully a fragile, old lady! What were the Darringtons thinking of? Another thought began to trouble her as she headed back to the sitting-room. How had they known about the shelter's finances?

Emma pushed the door open with her foot and then stopped dead in her tracks. She was just in time to see Martha's hand move hurriedly from her chest where it had been splayed out.

'Gran, are you feeling all right? Is there any pain in your chest?'

'No, it's a bit tight, that's all.'

'I'm going to call Dr Brennan.'

Ignoring Martha's plea not to make a fuss she went back into the hallway to make her call. She was assured that Dr Brennan, who was already on his rounds, would be contacted straight away.

Somewhat relieved, she returned to her grandmother.

'I managed to speak to Fiona at the surgery,' she told her. 'She seemed to think Dr Brennan could be with us quite quickly. There's no harm in having it checked up, Gran.'

The sound of the doorbell had Emma hurrying down the hallway and when she opened the door to find Dr Brennan facing her she gave immediate voice to her anxiety.

'Oh, Doctor, I'm so pleased you could come. I'm worried about Gran.'

As Emma led him down the hallway she was able to explain that her grandmother had had a clash with a visitor which had left her very upset and with some troubling symptoms. After she had taken him into the sitting-room she left them alone. Anxious moments followed as she busied herself in the kitchen, hardly able to keep her mind on the task in hand and then she was looking up as the kitchen door opened and Dr Brennan came in.

'You can rest easy in your mind, Emma. I've given your grandmother an examination and everything seems to be OK. I would guess that the tightness in the chest was due to tension and seems to have passed now.'

'Thank goodness! I was terribly worried.'

'Well, you were right to call me in. We can't afford to take risks. Of course it would be better if Mrs Holberry could avoid stress,' he said, 'but I know that's not always possible.'

He left, Emma's thanks ringing in his ears, and then she was closing the door and leaning against it, the relief his assurance had brought already being eclipsed by a nagging anxiety. Thanks to Bill Bryant's bullying tactics, Martha would now have to know everything about how close to disaster they had come. She had hoped to spare her that knowledge until her ill health was behind her.

'I've a good mind to go round there and give the Darringtons a piece of my mind,' she raged to Nigel that evening.

Martha was in bed and at Emma's suggestion they had stayed in and she had cooked them supper.

'Not only have they upset Gran,' she went on, 'but now I've to go through all the books with her. I've persuaded her to wait a few days until she's had a chance to recover from Bryant's visit but I fear she's going to get into another state when she discovers the full truth.'

'Perhaps it's time Martha was put in the picture. I never was too keen on keeping her in the dark in the first place.'

'That's not the point, Nigel. It should be up to me, her granddaughter, to decide such matters. I shouldn't be forced to act because of outside interference. I guess I'd better ring up for an appointment to meet one of the high-and-mighty Darringtons and put my complaint in person.'

'But you can't, darling. What I mean is that the Darringtons aren't there. The whole family's in the South of France. It was in the local rag the other week. You know, in that gossip column.'

'Really? Then who instructed Bryant to act as he did?'

'I guess he acted on his own initiative, and as he's not noted for his commonsense that's probably why he made such a hash of things. Look, darling, let me compose a suitable letter to the Darringtons, acting as your solicitor. I mean, we don't want to go throwing accusations around. It could land us in hot water.'

'I guess you're right,' Emma conceded. 'But I really would like to find out how they knew about our dreadful financial situation.'

'Things get around, darling. It happens.'

'But very few people knew the true state of affairs,' Emma persisted. 'Apart from ourselves, there's just Deborah and Jenny.'

'And that vet, Jenny's boyfriend.'

'Rick! But he's hardly likely to gossip about us.'

'It only needs a few careless words here and there.'

'I guess so. Only I just wonder what else the Darringtons know about us.'

Martha's condition remained quite stable over the next few days and Emma was able to concentrate on her design commission, so much so that Friday morning saw her delivering the completed work to the chief vet at Green's. When she left, the sun broke through, imitating her upbeat mood. The cheque which the chief vet had promptly handed over was the first payment she had received in a long while and it seemed as though her career had been handed back to her. She stood a moment, relishing the thought, and then, reluctant to go straight home, decided to revisit the coffee shop where she and Rick had celebrated before.

She might have known he'd be there. He was sitting alone and her mind warred between a desire to share this moment with a good friend and inherent caution warning her that she and Rick could never be just friends.

It's only a cup of coffee, hardly improper, she berated herself and she was just about to push the door open when, to her surprise, Bill Bryant appeared and sat down opposite Rick. She shrank away from the door. A group of people arrived to push their way into the coffee shop and Emma wandered off down the street, wondering about what she had just seen. Of course there was no reason why Rick shouldn't be friends with Bryant but could the leaks about their financial plight have come from him? Speculation was hopeless, she told herself as she headed off for where she had parked her car. She really would have to speak to him.

Emma was reluctant to visit him at the flat but she was just coming to the conclusion that she would have to do just that when Jenny presented her with the perfect opportunity.

Interrupted at her computer one afternoon, a flustered Jenny explained that Rick would be dropping by any minute for tea and she had to hurry down to the south field.

'I've got to separate Monty from the others. He's been acting up again.'

Monty, an irascible billy goat, often had to spend time on his own to calm down and, as Emma nodded her head knowingly, Jenny made a request.

'So could you hold the fort here with Rick until I get back?'

'Sure.'

As Jenny shot off, Emma shut down her computer and wandered through to the kitchen. After putting the kettle on, she assembled the tea things, managed to find enough biscuits to provide a selection and then set out the tray. She was just wondering how long she would have to wait when Rick arrived, looking surprised to see her.

'Jenny sends her apologies,' she said quickly. 'She'll be with us shortly but she's got to see to Monty first.'

'Condemned to solitary confinement again, is he?' Rick asked.

'I'm afraid so,' Emma told him with a smile.

He was standing beside her and, after handing over his cup, Emma moved to the armchair next to the fireplace.

For a few moments they drank in a companionable silence while Emma wondered how to say what she must, but it was Rick who spoke first.

'And how's your grandmother been since she left the nursing home?'

'She's out with Deborah at the moment and she's doing well in general but we did have rather an upset last week.'

'Really?'

'Bill Bryant just turned up out of the blue. Gran was on her own and he managed to upset her quite a lot. She was so stressed I had to send for the doctor but, fortunately, the effects wore off so she didn't have to be readmitted to hospital.'

'That must have been a relief for you. But what was Bill Bryant up to? It's not as though he has anything to do with the shelter.'

'The Darringtons are trying to buy us out. They want our land.'

Surprise fleeted across his face. That was news to him, Emma thought.

'Gran won't hear of it,' she explained, 'and didn't even reply to their letter. Bryant came for an answer, and what's worse is he taunted Gran with the state of our finances. I'd managed to keep Gran from knowing how bad things have been.'

'No wonder she was upset. Are you going to put in a complaint?'

'Nigel's drafting a letter for me, but what's rather disturbing is that I don't know how the Darringtons knew so much about our money problems.'

In a split second it was as though the implications of her words sank in and he turned a questioning face to her.

'Surely you don't think I was responsible.'

'Not deliberately, of course not. It's just that you know Bill Bryant and it's easy to let things slip.'

'Not in my case. I liaise with Bill about protecting the badger sett on the estate but I certainly don't gossip with him about my friends.'

If the briskly-spoken response hadn't signalled his annoyance the look on his face left Emma in no doubt that he had taken her words as a slur. Swiftly she tried to make amends.

'I'm sorry if that came out all wrong. I know you've always had our best interests at heart and I wouldn't want you to think . . . '

'Its OK, Emma, I get the picture.'

Now he was on his feet, his face turned away from hers.

'I really must be going. Thanks for

the tea. Give my apologies to Jenny.'

Then he was gone, and Emma was left fuming at herself, for the clumsy and inept way she had conducted the whole thing.

8

Over the next few days Emma's mood did not improve. How had she managed to alienate one of the people who had helped most? The look on Rick's face as she had asked her clumsy questions lingered in her memory. She threw herself into work at the shelter but the feeling persisted that she really had to see Rick and apologise for her suspicions.

When faced with his closed front door, however, her resolution nearly faltered and it took a moment to calm herself with a deep breath before she pressed the bell. Emma was just thinking that he must be out when the door swung open. There was surprise on Rick's face.

'Emma, how nice to see you.'

The words were perfunctory and there was no hint of warmth in his eyes.

'I'm sorry to arrive unannounced but after the other day I felt I had to speak to you, clear the air. Look, can I come in?'

'Sure.'

He stepped aside and Emma brushed past him to enter the small passageway. When they were both in the sitting-room she turned to face him but the words she was about to utter were unsaid when the kitchen door opened and Jenny appeared.

'Who was — oh, it's you Emma, how nice.'

She cast what Emma could only describe as a fond look at Rick.

'I'm cooking some supper for Rick, making sure he gets some home-cooked food for once. There's going to be plenty if you'd like to join us.'

'No, really, it's very kind of you but I've only dropped by for a quick word with Rick. I'm not stopping.'

'OK,' Jenny's casual response came. 'I'll get back to my cooking then.'

She disappeared, leaving them to

an uneasy silence.

'Jenny seems to think I need domesticating,' Rick said at last.

Women often do think that about men they are falling in love with, was Emma's thinking, but that sort of speculation wasn't what she was here for.

'Anyway,' she went on, 'I won't keep you from your supper. It's just that I wanted to apologise for what I said the other day. Anxiety over Gran must have completely muddled my thinking. I know you would never gossip about us to others, especially about something as sensitive as our financial situation. I was wrong to imply anything different.'

As a smile broke out on his face it was as though some inner tension had been released.

'I'm relieved to hear you say that, Emma. It was pretty disturbing to find that you thought I might have been working against you.'

Put so bluntly it did seem like a crazy charge.

'Well, I'm glad we've been able to sort things out.'

They were still standing facing each other and just as Emma was telling herself to pull her eyes away from his there came a clatter from the kitchen.

'I think Jenny might need some help,' Emma said. 'I'll show myself out.'

'Hang on, perhaps you'd like to join us for a drink.'

'No, thanks, I really need to be going.'

A cry of exasperation came from the kitchen and Emma was aware of Rick heading in that direction as she left the sitting-room. Once out in the open air, Emma's watch told her that she had quite some time to kill before she was due to meet Nigel. She set off walking, thinking over what had just occurred between herself and Rick. They seemed to have made peace, so that was good, wasn't it? Why, then, did she have this rather empty feeling? The cosy, domestic scene she had witnessed between Jenny and Rick couldn't possibly have anything to do with it, could it? The image of Jenny's open countenance as she looked admiringly at Rick continued to linger in her mind.

Her evening with Nigel was not a great success. He had brought along brochures of places offering wedding receptions and, as Emma looked at their grand façades, she simply couldn't see her friends fitting into such settings, still less her grandmother. When she put her concerns into words, though, Nigel put up a strong defence.

'Darling, I'm sure your friends and family would be happy to fit in with what we want. It's our day, after all.'

Quite, although it seemed to be a day that increasingly belonged to the Hamiltons rather than the Holberrys.

'I'm not sure,' Emma demurred. 'I want my family to feel comfortable.'

'And I'm sure they will, darling. After all, it'll be the most important event of our lives. We really do need a glamorous background to set it off.'

He turned his attention once more to his literature and, although Emma tried to show some enthusiasm, she couldn't help feeling that she was playing a part, that another person with her name was planning her wedding, and she was a mere onlooker.

About a week later, she was surprised to receive a call from Rick.

'Emma, hi. Look, I've been doing some digging into this business with the Darringtons and I've come up with something interesting. Can we meet for lunch tomorrow?'

'I guess so. Where do you suggest?'

He named a pub in a neighbouring village, they agreed on a time and then Emma was left to nurse her curiosity.

He was already there, ensconced in a corner, when she arrived the following day.

'Thanks for agreeing to meet me,' he said, pulling out a chair for her.

'Well, it all sounded so mysterious, I couldn't resist the invitation!'

He pulled a wry face.

'I hope my news meets your expectations then.'

He pulled his chair up closer to the table.

'I had a meeting with Bill Bryant a couple of days ago, just routine about badger protection and he let slip that the Darringtons are planning some sort of leisure development in the south west corner of the estate, holiday chalets, or some such, and Bill was given the task of checking whether or not the ancient badger sett ran underneath the site. If it had it would have blocked any development but it doesn't, to Bryant's evident relief.'

'But how does this relate to the sanctuary?'

'Just look at this a moment.'

Rick pulled a map out of his pocket and proceeded to unfold it on the table. It was an ordnance survey map of their neighbourhood and, as Emma pored over it, Rick stabbed at it with a forefinger.

'This is the south west corner of the

estate, more or less adjacent to your grandmother's property, which lies between it and a major road.'

Now understanding dawned on Emma.

'They want our land for an access road!'

'Exactly. Why else would they want to increase an already large estate? And it means that your land is very necessary to them.'

'Which was not reflected in the price offered,' was Emma's crisp rejoinder. 'Only standard agricultural prices were offered for the land, with quite a lot for the cottage.'

'No doubt a sweetener, to stop you probing any further.'

'As Gran turned it down flat we never had any reason to probe further.'

'But if I'm right about this, it might change Martha's mind. She could ask for a higher price, then build superior facilities for the animals elsewhere.'

'I'll tell her but I really don't think it'll make any difference. Honeysuckle

Cottage is her home and I don't think she could bear to move away.'

'It would be a massive undertaking, too, and could be detrimental to her health. I'm sure she's right to stay put.'

Emma found herself comparing Rick's reaction with Nigel's. Why couldn't her fiancé see beyond profit margins and give his wholehearted support to Martha's determination to remain?

'The Darringtons can't force you out, anyway,' Rick offered.

'It's just as well. Bill Bryant seemed to think that bullying might work, and look how much upset that caused.'

Rick folded up the map and slipped it back into his jacket pocket.

'Then let's forget all about the pesky Darringtons and choose our lunch.'

Emma found that she was starving and after they had chosen, Rick went to the bar to order. Emma thought how easily they had slipped back into their friendship. It was a relief that she had managed to bridge the gap between them. Being at odds with Rick had been an unsettling experience.

'The meal will be with us shortly.'

Rick was back by her side, holding two drinks.

'Shall we escape from this dark corner and find a spot outside?'

'Good idea.'

She rose, scooping up her jacket and bag at the same time.

Outside, they found a terrace edged by rose bushes. Petals which had dropped from the full, open blooms littering the crazy paving. It was a sign that September was advancing, leaving the summer well behind.

'Only two more weeks and Jenny will be back at university,' she said.

'You'll miss her.'

'We certainly will although she's promised to come in at weekends. And, thankfully, Deborah seems to have become a permanent fixture. I can't tell you how grateful I am for how you brought us together.'

'I'm just glad it worked out. And

what about your own career? Any more commissions on the horizon?'

'Hopefully. I'm seeing a prospective client in Summerton next week.'

'Good luck with that.'

'I guess your thoughts are already turning to your departure.'

'Not really. Busy vets don't have too much time to think. Besides, it's still a few months away. I won't be leaving until after Christmas.'

And what sort of a Christmas was Jenny going to have this year? For a split second Emma could almost feel the desolation Rick's leaving would bring to her young friend. The waitress arrived with their meals and when they began to eat, the conversation became general, Rick amusing her with tales of some of his more awkward patients. Then it was time for Rick to return to his rounds and for Emma to head back to the shelter.

Over tea with Martha later she relayed what Rick had found out, and the reaction was entirely predictable.

'It makes no difference to me what they want my land for. They still can't have it.'

'But don't you see what this means, Gran? With the Darringtons needing your land so badly you could negotiate a much higher price.'

'No amount of money will make me leave my home, Emma.'

'OK, Gran, if that's what you want, you know I'll back you.'

Several days later, Emma was interrupted in the parlour by a worried-looking Deborah.

'I've just attempted to put in an order with Dawson Brothers but they've refused to accept it until we've cleared our outstanding debt. I promised to see to it but when I checked the accounts it's down as being paid.'

'Dawson Brothers,' Emma repeated, something stirring in her memory. 'I remember now,' she announced. 'That was one of the bills Nigel promised to clear. He's terribly busy at work at the moment so he must have simply forgotten. I'll call the Dawsons right now and pay with my credit card, only we don't want to alienate them. They're one of our best suppliers.'

She went through to the office and, her task done, turned her attention back to Deborah.

'There, all straightened out. Mr Dawson will see to our order right away.'

'Good,' Deborah murmured, adding, 'I hope that's the only unpaid bill we've got to contend with. It'll throw our budget right out if there are more.'

'Well, I'm seeing Nigel for lunch tomorrow so I'll check with him.'

Emma had arranged to meet Nigel at his office but when she arrived she was told by Miss Burnett that he had been delayed at a client's home and would be along shortly.

'Oh, well, I guess I'll just wait in his room.'

'But Mr Hamilton doesn't like anyone to be in there unattended.'

'I'm sure that doesn't apply to his

fiancée,' Emma replied tartly before pushing open his office door and sweeping past Miss Burnett.

Once inside, she allowed a smile to break out on her face. It wasn't often she was able to claim even a small victory over Nigel's strong-willed secretary. She crossed over to the window, spent a few moments watching people scurrying by, glanced at her watch and then turned to rest against the window ledge, her restless gaze taking in every corner of the office.

With its solid furniture, law books shelved in a glass cabinet and an oatmeal carpet it must look like the offices of solicitors all over the country, Emma mused. Immaculate, too, unlike his desk. Her glance fell to the untidy jumble of folders on it and her hand automatically reached out to straighten them, until she saw what was written in Nigel's distinctive printing on one of them — Holberry Animal Sanctuary.

She lifted the folder up to the light and opened it. Inside was a bundle of invoices and as she glanced at them she realised that these were the bills Nigel had promised to settle. Nothing had been written on them to suggest they had been paid so she had been right in her supposition that, under pressure of work, he had simply forgotten. She'd better mention it as soon as he arrived. There was something else in there, too, a folded white sheet, and when she pulled it out she had to spread it out on the desk in order to scrutinise it.

What she saw almost stopped her breath. It was a draft planning application for the Darrington estate. Holiday chalets were marked out in the south western corner, just as Rick had surmised, and he had been right in his other supposition, too. There was an access road going right through the sanctuary! Nigel had known about this all along! That's why he had been pressurising her to persuade her grandmother to sell.

The door opened and she heard Nigel's cheery greeting.

'Hi, darling, sorry I'm late only Mrs Dukes insisted I stay for tea and you know what old ladies are like. Anyway . . . '

He broke off when he caught sight of her face. He closed the door behind him and stepped farther into the room.

'What's the matter, darling? You look as though you've seen a ghost.'

Emma straightened and it was as though someone else was speaking.

'Not a ghost, just something that makes me think you're not the man I thought you were,' she said coldly.

Moving closer, he could now see what she had been poring over and his cheeks suddenly reddened.

'That's confidential, Emma. You shouldn't be looking in there.'

The cheek of the man! Indignation firing her speech, Emma rattled out, 'The dossier had our name on it. I thought I had a right to look, and it's a bit rich you accusing me of unethical behaviour.'

She stabbed a finger on the right

hand corner of the document.

'This has your firm's address on it. You were involved in this when you were trying to persuade me to back a sale. How ethical was that?'

'No, that's not true. If this deal goes ahead our firm will get the conveyancing work but no-one has yet been assigned to it. There's no conflict of interest, Emma, and you can't say there is.'

'But you were hoping to get the assignment, weren't you?' she said. 'It would put you in a good position to get the partnership you crave.'

She could see her words had struck home and, for a moment, Nigel looked distinctly rattled, then he struck a defiant note.

'And what if I did want a good future for myself? Why is that such a crime? It was for our joint future, Emma.'

'At Gran's expense? Do you think I would ever agree to that?'

'Martha would have got a good deal. It was in her interest, too.'

'If Gran had accepted their offer she would have taken less than the land value. The Darringtons forgot to mention that our land was essential to a commercial development, something that would have pushed its price up.'

'Now, hold on.'

A worried look was back on Nigel's face.

'I had nothing to do with sales negotiations.'

'You were happy to go along with the deception, weren't you? Doubtless you were too scared of upsetting the Darringtons to play fair with us.'

'You're making everything sound very unsavoury. I can assure you there's been no professional misconduct.'

'Oh, Nigel, I'm not going to put in a complaint against you. What do you take me for? It's the way you betrayed my trust that bothers me, not your professional conduct.'

He looked only slightly less anxious.

'Everything I've done has been for us, Emma, for a prosperous start to our married life.'

In that split second, as she looked at him, it was as though she was facing a stranger. She thought her voice might break but it sounded remarkably strong as she put her thoughts into words.

'There will be no married life for us, Nigel. Do you think I could be with a man who has betrayed my family?'

The ring slid off her finger easily and as she placed it on the desk she scooped up the pile of unpaid bills with her other hand. The exchange seemed to signify what her choice really meant, an uncertain future balancing the books at the shelter instead of the comfortable, secure life as Nigel's wife. So be it, her decision was made.

As she strode towards the door, he moved to detain her.

'Emma, you can't! You can't throw everything away after one row, one silly misunderstanding.'

'I think the misunderstanding has lasted all the time I have known you,

Nigel. Although our backgrounds are very different I always thought we had enough in common to bind us together. I now realise I was just deluding myself. It's not just background, Nigel. We seem to inhabit completely different worlds.'

Even now she could see no spark of remorse in his eyes, but why should she? She'd no doubt that Nigel had convinced himself, all along, that he had acted in both their interests. He continued to protest as she headed for the door but she didn't even pause as she twisted the knob and strode out.

During the drive back to the sanctuary she had an almost detached feeling, as though this was all happening to someone else. Why did she feel so frozen, so bereft of feeling? Surely she should feel some grief for her broken engagement.

Arriving back at the cottage, she let herself in and registered a mental vote of thanks that Deborah and her grandmother were out. She really didn't want to face anyone right now. The door to the parlour was half open and her hand had just reached out to push it wider when it was stilled by the sight of Rick and Jenny. Quite oblivious to her, they were seated on the small sofa, Jenny's head resting on his shoulder and Rick's arm around her, a look of such tenderness on his face that something churned inside Emma, an emotion she was quite unable to define.

Turning round, she crept back down the passage and slipped out of the door, closing it gently behind her. She needed to walk. She set off briskly for the south field. She came to an abrupt halt at the five-bar gate and leaned against it, looking at the grazing goats without really seeing them. Instead she saw the look on Rick's face as he had cradled Jenny. That's what she had lost in the space of a lunchtime visit to Nigel's office, someone to call her own, someone to provide the sort of safe haven she had craved for in her formative years trying to keep up with her rootless parents. Her belief that Nigel had been the man to do all that had proved to be a cruel delusion and, right now, she felt terribly alone.

9

'Although he'd never admit it I think it must have been Nigel who leaked information to the Darringtons about our finances,' Emma was telling Deborah whose eyes rose heavenwards.

'Emma, you poor thing! This is an awful lot to take in about your fiancé.'

'Except that he isn't my fiancé any more,' Emma reminded her. 'Things were all right between us when I was an up-and-coming graphic designer, hungry for success, but as soon as I took over this place, tensions surfaced. He just couldn't understand why anyone would dedicate themselves to animal rejects when there was no money or status in it. He must have seen the Darrington offer as heaven sent, a way to further his own career as well as extricate his future wife from a failing enterprise. That must have been why he didn't settle these.'

She spread the sheaf of invoices out on the table, and then pointed to a leaf of notepaper with a number written on it.

'I've paid what I can using my credit card but this is the total of what's still owing.'

'That does throw out the accounts!' Deborah exclaimed.

'And I've no resources left to fall back on.'

'Then we'll just have to think of a good money-making wheeze.'

Emma knew Deborah was putting a brave face on for her benefit and felt gratitude well up inside her. Coping with the collapse of her romantic dreams was difficult enough, she didn't think she could have dealt with the financial repercussions without her friend's aid.

'I'd been toying with the idea of having an autumn fair. Now I definitely think we should have one! Let me jot some ideas down on paper and then we'll talk them through,' Deborah was saying.

'That sounds wonderful. Organising a big event will help to take my mind off what's happened, too,' was Emma's rueful comment as she scooped the invoices back into a manila folder, then she turned back to her friend with a request. 'I'd be grateful if you didn't repeat what I've said about Nigel to anyone else. If anything got out it would jeopardise his professional reputation and, in spite of what's happened, I wouldn't want that.'

Deborah was quick with her reassurance.

'I do understand. I won't breath a word, but how will you explain your break-up to Martha?'

'Gran's never been too enthusiastic about my engagement. I think she'll be too busy celebrating to ask too many questions!'

Emma's assessment proved correct.

'I knew that interfering Anna Hamilton would ruin the whole thing in the end,' Martha gloated.

'It was nothing to do with Nigel's mother,' Emma declared, in an attempt to prevent a further blackening of Anna Hamilton's name. 'It's just that I realised that Nigel and I wanted very different things from life and that didn't bode well for our future happiness.'

'Well, he certainly looked down on what we were doing here,' was Martha's shrewd comment, 'and he would have made sure you were no longer a part of it if you had got married. I'm sure you've done the right thing, Emma. Better to face a broken engagement than an unhappy marriage.'

'Of course.'

Many people, she knew, would come up with similar sentiments over the next few days, and they were right, but kind words wouldn't banish the sense of failure she was now subject to, or restore her shattered self-confidence.

'I'm such a wimp,' she wailed to Deborah later, when they were having afternoon tea. 'I know what a rat Nigel was. I don't want the engagement back, truly I don't, but I'm still struggling to cope with it all. I feel so alone!'

'Emma, your trust was betrayed by the man who professed to love you! You won't recover from such a blow in an instant. It's bound to take time, and it's no use pretending it's going to be easy. This will be a lonely time for you, especially as I'm the only one to know all the details. Perhaps it would help to confide in someone else.'

An open countenance with dark eyes that could be storm tossed one minute and lit by undisguised mirth the next crept into her mind. It would be so tempting to pour out all her troubles to Rick, to lean on the strength she knew was in him and let his sympathy act as a balm, but she couldn't do it. And she must constantly remind herself of the sight of Jenny in his arms.

'There's no-one I can speak to. I have to deal with this in my own way. Now let's get to work and check through the proposals for the autumn fair.'

Their heads bowed once more to the task in hand.

A few days later, Emma was pouring dog food into the feeding bowls and, engrossed in her work, failed to sense that anyone was behind her until a hand dropped lightly on her shoulder. She spun round, to find herself facing Rick. He stepped back abruptly.

'Sorry if I startled you. I called out but you didn't seem to hear.'

'Too busy rattling these.'

She held up the packet of biscuits, and then there was an awkward pause. It occurred to her that this was the first time they'd met since she'd broken off her engagement. She was now free, but he wasn't.

'Look, I . . . '

He cleared his throat and began again.

'I've heard that you've called off your wedding and I just wanted to say that I know you must be going through a very difficult time right now, and that I'm here if you need anything.'

In his face she saw a message of sympathy that made her heart turn over. Her throat tight with pent-up emotion, she pushed the words out.

'I do appreciate that, really I do, and . . . '

It was no use. The threatened tears could no longer be held back and when they began to roll down her cheeks, Rick's arms went round her and she was pulled against his broad chest. His hand stroked her hair, he murmured low-voiced words of comfort and Emma found herself weeping her heart out. She had no real idea how long the emotional storm lasted but when, at last, she eased herself out of his embrace, scarlet-faced, she offered an apology.

'I'm so sorry! I'd no right to collapse in a heap like that. You must think me a complete fool.'

Her eyes widened as she saw the damp patch on his denim shirt.

'And I've made a complete mess of your shirt!'

Automatically her hand splayed out on the moistened patch and through the fabric she could feel the heat of his skin, and the tell-tale beat of his racing heart. Her hand pulled back as though she had touched fire.

Looking down, he dismissed her concerns.

'It's nothing. You've no need to apologise, for anything.'

Incisive dark eyes switched back to her face.

'Did that help, Emma?'

'Yes, it did.'

She had longed to tell Rick everything but had convinced herself that she must curb her tongue. In the event, what had just happened had not broken her resolution but a wordless exchange had acted as a catalyst, allowing her to vent emotions she had kept bottled up.

'Remarkably, I haven't cried since the break-up happened,' she told him. 'I think it was long overdue, and I do feel better.'

'I'm so glad,' he replied with smile.

'That's what friends are for.'

'Of course.'

'If you can hang on for a few moments I can make us some coffee after I've put the food out.'

She sensed a swift glance down at his watch.

'Afraid I'll have to say no. I should have been at my next appointment about ten minutes ago.'

'Oh, well, thanks for dropping by then.'

The words seemed so banal after the moment of closeness they had just shared and Rick seemed to feel that, too, his expression hesitant as he showed no signs of leaving.

'I guess you'd better set off as you're running so late,' she reminded him.

'Yes, right. I'll see you soon, Emma.'

He left, and Emma began setting out the food for her hungry charges and, as she did so, marvelled at how much more cheerful she felt. She knew that one weeping session wasn't enough to sweep away all the disappointment she was feeling but it was as though the cloud which seemed to hover over her had lifted a little. The healing process had begun.

The date for the autumn fair was set and during the countdown to the big day the shelter became a hive of a activity. Much of the preparation work was divided between Emma, Deborah and a much-improved Martha. Deborah and Martha used their contacts in the voluntary sector to drum up support and ensure there would be a good range of stalls for the day whilst Emma sought sponsorship from local firms and was in charge of publicity. At their first progress meeting she also had some good news for them.

'Remember Carrie Brown whom I was at school with?' she asked, addressing her grandmother. 'Well, she's now head groom at Dappledown stables and she's persuaded the owner to let her bring over some ponies.'

'Pony rides!' Martha's eyes lit up.

'The children will love that.'

'Yes, and she's got a Shetland that'll be ideal for the little ones. All the proceeds will come to us, too. I think the owner is quite happy just to get some publicity out of it.'

'We need more attractions for children,' Deborah remarked.

'You're right.' Emma's brow furrowed. 'We've got plenty of land available so why not have some bouncy castles, helter-skelters, that sort of thing? There are plenty of commercial operators who will happily rent a pitch from us. I'll look into it if you like.'

This was agreed and, later, as Emma was making notes of what had been decided, it struck her that, only a short time ago, Martha would have balked at turning the shelter into a vulgar fairground! Finding out how close they had come to ruin had made Martha much more realistic about funding, Emma mused, which had made it easier to get agreement for what needed to be done. Here Deborah's influence had been crucial. Her grandmother had so much respect for her that she was always willing to listen to her advice.

The day of the fair dawned clear and bright, the nip of autumn in the air disguised by the strong rays of sun which shone from a blue sky dotted with fluffy white clouds. Emma's spirits were as high as those clouds as she helped Carrie lead her ponies down the ramp of the horsebox.

'We're going to have a wonderful day,' she enthused to her friend.

'I'm going to enjoy myself, anyway,' Carrie declared. 'It's a real treat to get away from routine at the stables.'

Experienced with horses, Emma had opted to help Carrie out and was put in charge of the Shetland, a chestnut named Scamp.

'His name just about describes his nature,' Carrie warned. 'He's inclined to nip if he's in a grumpy mood.'

'Don't worry, I'll show him who's boss,' Emma promised.

Another volunteer arrived to help

Carrie with the main pony rides and soon they had the ponies tethered and hay nets organised.

'Now it's time to see to ourselves,' Carrie declared, retrieving a vacuum flask and plastic cups from her rucksack.

They sat on the grass, chatting and gulping down hot coffee. Then as soon as the fair was officially opened they were inundated with families wanting rides for their offspring. Whilst Carrie and her helper took out two ponies at a time, Emma, as she was dealing with very young children, just took out Scamp. Tiny tots, their faces alive with laughter, clung on to his shaggy mane as Emma led him around the field at a gentle pace.

The morning seemed to fly by and it was well after one o'clock when Carrie strolled over.

'I'll take over here and you can grab something to eat,' she suggested. 'I'll have my lunch when you get back.'

'OK. I won't be long.'

Apart from the hunger pangs now

gnawing away at her stomach, Emma also welcomed the chance to have a look at how things were going throughout the rest of the fair. As she made her way back to Honeysuckle Cottage, all the signs were encouraging. There were plenty of people milling about, the atmosphere was decidedly festive and Deborah, presiding over the tombola, seemed to share this view, presenting a triumphant thumbs-up gesture as Emma passed by her.

Now she was nearing the marquee where Rick was giving talks on pet welfare. He must have just broken off for lunch, she guessed, catching sight of a sign which stated that the next talk would be at two. Perhaps he could join her at the cottage. She was standing and hesitating a moment when a hand on her shoulder had her starting, then spinning around.

'Jenny! How lovely to see you. It's been ages!'

They had hardly seen Jenny since she had returned to college and Emma had missed her young friend.

'Oh, I know I've been neglecting you and I'm sorry,' she wailed, 'but everything's gone crazy in my life!'

She saw the alarm on Emma's face and hastened to reassure her.

'Oh, nothing bad, quite the reverse.'

She paused a moment, as though building herself up, and the look of joy on her face almost stopped Emma's breath.

'I'm in love, he loves me, and I thought it would never happen, but it has!' she announced.

'Oh, I'm so glad for you, really I am.'

Was it really her speaking those words, Emma wondered, or had a polite stranger just taken over her body?

Not appearing to notice anything amiss, Jenny's attention was now taken by a group of young people who were calling and gesticulating to her.

'I'm here with the gang and they seem anxious to be off,' she explained hurriedly to Emma, 'so I'd better go.'

She deposited a kiss on Emma's cheek.

'Take care and I hope we get a chance to talk soon.'

Emma mumbled a suitable response but when Jenny left did not follow her example of rushing off. Somehow she could not take her eyes off the entrance to the marquee and the sign above it emblazed with the name of Rick Delayne. So, Jenny's romantic dreams had come to fruition whilst hers had foundered on deceit and betrayal. A feeling of despair, fiercer and deeper than she had ever experienced, filled her from top to toe. Jenny had finally won the love of the man she adored — Rick Delayne, the man Emma also loved!

Afterwards, Emma was to marvel at how her heart had suddenly opened to reveal its secret at last. In the past she had closed her mind to its whispered message, throwing herself even more into her relationship with Nigel in the hope of extinguishing doubts. Circumstances had freed her from her promise to Nigel but, bruised and bewildered she had been unable to look searchingly at her innermost feelings. Now, Jenny's bombshell had forced her to do just that and she could see the truth for the first time. The attraction she had always felt for Rick, and fought, had gone far deeper than she had supposed.

For the rest of the day, Emma just went through the motions, continuing with her duties whilst her mind was in a ferment. Everyone else was too busy, thankfully, to notice anything amiss and at the close of the event, it was Emma who volunteered to do the accounts, fearful of leaving herself unoccupied and prey to disturbing thoughts.

As she finished her task, just before midnight, she could comfort herself with the thought that the takings for the day would pay for the unexpected, unpaid bills Nigel's treachery had landed them with. Her personal life might be wrecked but at least the shelter was out of the woods again. That was her final sleepy thought as she crawled, exhausted, into bed.

Over the following week, Emma did her best to come to terms with the changed situation but the smudges beneath her eyes and listless air, much commented on by Deborah, were testimony to the fact that, the more she tried, the harder it seemed to be getting. She had mentally steeled herself for her first meeting with Rick ever since discovering her true feelings for him but was quite taken aback, one afternoon, on her return from Summerton, to find him and Deborah in the parlour.

'Hello, you two,' was her greeting as she busied herself unloading carrier bags on to the sofa.

It was a useful ploy, giving her a moment to steady her racing heart, but by the time she returned her attention to them, it was racing even faster!

Deborah did not seem to notice anything untoward.

'Come and look at this,' she suggested. 'Rick's come up with rather an interesting proposal.'

Now Emma noticed they had the local ordnance survey map spread out on the table and, as Emma seated herself, Rick said, 'I've been doing a bit of thinking, about the Darrington development and their wish to buy up your land for an access road. As we know, that's a non-starter, but there is one way in which they can get their access road and you get to keep most of your land, as well as make a good deal of money for the shelter.'

Emma's widened eyes followed his right index finger as he traced a route on the map.

'If an access road was to take the route I'm marking out, all you would lose would be part of the south field and the money brought in would allow you to build a new kennel block, as well as put some capital away to form a trust fund for long-term stability.'

Long-term stability! It was what they had often longed for at Holberry Animal Sanctuary and never achieved. Could it possibly be won now? Turning a questioning face to her friend, Emma could tell from the light in her eyes and air of contained excitement that Deborah was sold on the idea.

'Do you think this could work?'

'I do,' she confirmed, then turning to Rick, she put a question. 'But are you sure the Darringtons will welcome this proposal?'

'I know they're desperate to get this development off the ground but we won't know for sure until we make a formal approach.'

'Then we'll need a solicitor,' Emma said, speaking her thoughts aloud.

There was an awkward silence which Deborah hurried to break.

'The people I use are very good. I'm sure they'll represent us.'

There was agreement and then Emma moved the discussion on.

'Then all we've got to do is persuade Gran to agree to all this.'

'That's where you come in,' Rick said. 'We think you're the best person to persuade her.'

'I disagree.'

Turning to Deborah she made a suggestion.

'Gran has enormous respect for your judgement so let's both speak to her. I'm sure that'll give us the best chance of success.'

Deborah was happy to comply.

'That's fine with me. We'll talk to her as soon as possible.'

'Well, you ladies seem to have it all in hand,' Rick said.

He rose, and then addressed Emma directly.

'Perhaps you'll give me a call?'

She deliberately withdrew her gaze.

'Sure, or Deborah will.'

The less contact she had with Rick the better. Her face averted from his, she didn't see the look which passed over his face but Deborah did and when he had gone she tried some gentle probing.

'Has there been some sort of a falling out between you and Rick? You seemed much more distant than usual with him just now.'

'No, of course not.'

Emma looked down at the map in front of them and opted for an abrupt change of subject.

'Let's talk through what we're going to say to Gran.'

In the event, they faced little opposition from Martha. Seared by her knowledge of how close they had come to ruin, she was surprisingly open to a radical suggestion and once her concerns had been answered gave her approval for an approach to be made to the Darringtons.

After that, everything seemed to happen very quickly. Deborah's lawyers were instructed to act for the Holberrys and their initial approach to the Darringtons was greeted positively. Many weeks of negotiation would be needed but once the process had started Emma allowed herself some cautious optimism that soon, the animal shelter would gain the sort of financial security which would ensure its future. It was a wonderful prospect but, however much satisfaction it might bring, nothing could lessen the heartache caused by losing the man she loved.

Work seemed to be the only remedy to keep the pain at bay and, after an early start to the day one morning, Emma had just returned wearily to the cottage for a longed-for cup of coffee when she disturbed Deborah in the parlour. At the sight of her she started.

'Oh, Emma, there you are! I've just finished my drink but there's a full pot of coffee here.'

She gestured with her left hand but Emma noticed that with her right she was surreptitiously sliding a newspaper beneath a pile of documents. Then she stood up abruptly.

'Well, better be getting on. I've got Rick in to see to Sid's kennel cough.'

She hurried off, leaving Emma somewhat puzzled. What was going on? Seating herself at the table she retrieved the hidden newspaper and began to scan it. It took a moment to find what Deborah must have seen, and then two names jumped out at her. An engagement was announced, between Nigel Hamilton and Sarah Burnett. Nigel was going to marry his secretary!

She began to shake uncontrollably and barely noticed when the door opened until a voice, a deeply-loved voice, spoke.

'Oh, my darling, I'm so sorry, but it will get better, I promise you.'

She took the tissue offered by Rick but when she turned to face him, she saw the look on his face change from concern to bewilderment as he realised that she was laughing, not crying. As she wiped her dampened eyes, she offered an explanation.

'I know this is a crazy, nervous sort of reaction but it seems so absurdly right that Nigel should marry his soulless, super-efficient secretary!'

Rick's head went from side to side.

'No sooner had the guy broken off with you than he was appearing everywhere with this woman. I thought he'd cheated on you.'

'I broke things off, for good reason. It's a long story but I realised that I'd never truly loved Nigel and I was well out of it.'

She turned aside before she could say too much but the next moment Rick had pulled her round to face him.

'Then why did you keep me at such a distance? I thought you needed space to recover from your hurt.'

'How could I take you from Jenny?'

At last she must speak the truth.

'I couldn't seek my own happiness at the expense of someone else's feelings.'

'Take me from Jenny?' he repeated. 'Surely you don't think . . . '

He took both her hands in his and looked her full in the face.

'Listen to me, Emma. Jenny and I have always been friendly. She's a great kid, but we've never been involved. How could anything happen between us when I was eating my heart out over you?'

He loved her! The words sang through her, almost unscrambling her thoughts, as the words tumbled out.

'Oh, Rick, I thought I'd never hear anything like that from you. When I met Jenny at the autumn fair and she said she was so much in love.'

'You put two and two together and came up with the wrong answer,' he cut in. 'I saw Jenny, too, that day and she told me that she'd recently become reconciled with the young man she'd split up with just before the summer break. I was so pleased for her, but I couldn't help wondering if there would ever be a happy ending for me.'

The look he now gave her caused Emma's heart to tilt.

'Well, my darling, will there be?'

'Oh, yes! I love you, Rick Delayne, with all my heart.'

It was exhilarating to speak the truth at last, almost as exhilarating as the kiss that followed, and later, much later, they began to discuss their future.

'I can hardly ask you to just walk off

into an African sunset,' Rick said, his brow furrowed. 'I mean there's Martha to consider, and I know how you feel about living abroad.'

'Enough.'

The command was gently spoken, the finger she had laid against his lips stopping his words.

'Rick, listen to me. I want to be with the man I love and if that means my future lies overseas, so be it. As for Gran, well, with Deborah here I know she'll be in safe hands. And I'm sure she'll approve,' she said, adding a provocative broadside, 'as long as there's a wedding on the horizon!'

'Emma, you're shameless! You've stolen my lines!'

His expression sobered suddenly as he captured her hands once more, his eyes holding hers.

'Emma, my love, I thought for so long that I would never be able to speak these words to you, but will you marry me and spend the rest of your days with me?'

'Do you know,' she said, 'when you moved into my flat I thought I'd found the perfect tenant.'

She returned her gaze to his and the message he saw there almost stopped his breath.

'But I'd no idea I'd also found the perfect husband.'

'I'll take that as a yes,' he returned, joy lighting his face as he reached for her once more.

THE END